BET YOUR HEART ON ME

SEASONED ROMANCE SERIES

BOOK ONE

ELIZABETH KELLY

EK PUBLISHING INC.

BET YOUR HEART ON ME

Finding love in your forties isn't easy…

Especially when you have a long to-do list. Running a small business and mending her broken relationship with her son are Hazel's top priorities.

Until Hendrix Smith walks into her flower shop.

He's smart, sexy, and confident, and Hazel can't deny their instant connection.

A flower shop was the last place Hendrix expected to find love. But the moment he meets Hazel, he can't resist her. She's beautiful, passionate, and intelligent. Asking her out is a no-brainer.

There's only one problem – their kids are dating.

For Hazel and Hendrix, ignoring their connection proves impossible. When their blossoming love strains Hazel's fragile relationship with her son, reality comes crashing in.

Now Hazel is caught between the two people she loves most. How can she choose between her love for her child and her love for Hendrix when either decision will shatter her heart?

CHAPTER 1

"Hazel, we need to talk."

"This sounds ominous." Hazel cut off a section of stem from the carnation and added the flower to the bouquet. She cocked her head and studied the flowers before reaching for another carnation.

When there was no reply, she glanced up at Indie. "What?"

Her best friend took a deep breath. "There's no easy way to tell you this, and, honestly, I wanted to wait to tell you when Sierra was with us, but, well... I think you need to know now. Especially with how much light is coming through the window."

Indie motioned to the large glass window to their left. The sun streamed through the glass, filling the flower shop with warm light. Hazel sighed. The natural light was gorgeous, but it also showcased how much the painted window sign had begun to peel. If the 'e' and the 'r' peeled much more, customers would start thinking her shop was called 'The Flow Pot'.

She mentally added 'repaint sign' to her already overflowing to-do list and cut the stem of the second carnation. "Before we have this serious talk, can I say thank you again for helping me today? Today is your only day off, and I can't tell you how much I appreciate you covering for Carlos. They hated having to bail on me, but their grandmother is being moved to the nursing home today, and they wanted to be there for her."

"You know I don't mind," Indie said. "Is it always this busy on Sundays?"

Hazel nodded. The shop was having a rare slow moment, but from the moment she'd opened at ten, there'd been customers in and out of the store. "Yeah, Sundays are busy, plus I always have a ton of bouquets to make for the week, so having someone here to man the cash register is a godsend."

"Happy to help." Indie leaned against the counter.

"What is it we need to talk about?" Hazel asked.

"Chin hairs," Indie said. "Specifically, your chin hairs. You need to tweeze or wax those suckers."

Hazel touched her chin. "What? They're not that bad."

"Oh, honey," Indie said, "you're in chin hair denial."

Hazel peered at her reflection in the glass counter, her fingers roaming over her chin. "I didn't think they were that noticeable."

Indie pointed to the glass window again. "The sun is lighting up your beard like a halo, my friend."

"Beard?" Hazel said.

"Slight exaggeration," Indie said. "Still, as your best friend, it's my duty to tell you that you need to tweeze."

"Thanks, I think." Hazel touched her chin again. "Of all the things I thought I'd be doing in my forties, plucking my chin hairs wasn't one of them."

"You and me both, girl." Indie plopped her curvy body down on the stool behind the counter. "I found a random white hair growing out of my forehead the other day. It was six inches long, Hazel. I swear. I only knew it was there because Twig was batting at it while I tried to sleep."

"That explains the scratch on your forehead," Hazel said.

Indie touched the scratch. "Yeah. Twig's kind of a monster."

"Kind of?" Hazel said. "I still can't figure out why you let that cat into your house. You know he's gonna murder you in your sleep, right?"

"Oh, totally," Indie said. "But I felt bad for him when they brought him into the clinic. It's not his fault he's angry."

The bell over the door jingled, and a group of women in their twenties stepped into the shop. Hazel smiled at them as they walked to a cooler and studied the flower bouquets inside.

"Oh, to have an ass that young and tight again," Indie said. "Of course, I never really had a tight ass. But my tits… now they were spectacular."

"Still are," Hazel said. "That guy who came in before lunch practically drooled on them."

"I considered giving him my number," Indie said.

Hazel laughed. "He must have been close to seventy."

"So what? I'm close to fifty."

"Forty-five is not close to fifty," Hazel said.

"Easy for you to say. You're younger than me."

"By three months," Hazel said.

Indie slid off the stool and straightened her t-shirt. "I'll see if the lovely young ladies with their perfect young bodies need some assistance."

Hazel laughed. "Just remember – your tits are better than theirs."

As Indie chatted with the women, Hazel added the final touches to the bouquet before covering it with plastic wrap.

She carried it to the second cooler at the back of the store and added it to the shelf with the others as the front bell jingled again. She still had two more custom bouquets to finish, and she really should reorder more –

"Excuse me?"

A deliciously deep voice spoke to her right, and she turned, her 'how can I help you' smile faltering as she took in the man standing beside her.

No, not a man. A god. A dark-haired, blue-eyed, perfect amount of silver in his hair, god.

"Hi." Her voice was breathy like she'd just taken herself for a lovely ride on the god standing before her. A ride that ended with the best orgasm of her life.

"Hello." He smiled at her, and she reached a hand behind her to steady herself on the glass cooler, fingerprints be damned.

When she didn't say anything else, confusion crossed his face. He glanced at the apron she wore with "The Flower Pot" stitched across it. "You work here, right?"

"I do," she said. "How can I help you?"

She still sounded breathy and uneven. She cleared her throat and, mindful of the chin hairs, made sure she wasn't standing in the beams of sunshine that reached the back of the store.

"Flowers," he said. "I need flowers."

He smiled at her, those even white teeth making her wonder what it might be like to have them nipping at her thighs.

"I have flowers," she said.

He laughed. "Probably why you work in a flower shop, huh?"

She giggled. Not a cute, I'm sexy, and I know it, giggle,

but a high-pitched, teetering right on the edge of a fairy tale witch cackle.

Groaning inwardly, her face beaming so brightly it probably highlighted every one of her unfortunate chin hairs, she cut off the cackle/giggle with the finely cut blade of self-preservation.

She was terrible at flirting, always had been. Even if she were a master of flirting like Sierra, the god standing before her would be married. Of course, he would. He looked to be around her age, and men her age were either married, gay, or going through a midlife crisis and dating women half their age.

No ring.

Her gaze had dropped to his ring finger without her even realizing it. He might have been gay, but more likely, he was bedding a different woman every night. Women who didn't have muffin-tops or wide hips or tits that pointed depressingly downward.

"Ma'am?" The god looked concerned and reached out to touch her forearm. It was a brief touch meant to prod her out of her inner thoughts, but it sent flickers of hungry need from her stomach to her pelvis. What would it feel like to have those rough fingertips sliding between her thighs? Tracing circles around her nipples?

Speaking of nipples… hers had pebbled, and thank fucking God for the apron she wore because her bra and thin t-shirt were not enough to hide her sudden arousal.

"Ma'am?" The god looked around, probably wondering if she was having a sudden stroke or a heart attack.

"Hazel," she said before he could call 9-1-1. "My name is Hazel, not ma'am."

He grinned, making the fine lines around his eyes deepen

and producing the faintest hint of a dimple in his left cheek. She wanted to lick it.

"Sorry, force of habit. I'm Hendrix."

Even his name was cool.

"Nice to meet you," she said. "What kind of flowers are you looking for?"

"I'm not sure," he said.

Used to the answer, she rattled off the first of her usual questions. "Does your girlfriend have a favourite flower?"

"Not for a girlfriend," he said.

"Oh. Boyfriend?"

He shook his head. "It's more of a work thing."

"All right. What are the colours in the office? Sometimes matching flowers to the office colours is a great choice when you aren't trying to say something specific with the flower gift."

"I'm trying to say something specific," he said.

She gave him a *go on* look. He looked uncomfortable now, a slight flush rising in his cheeks as he rubbed at the nape of his neck. "Do you have anything that says, 'I'm sorry I nearly set your house on fire'?"

She blinked at him. "Tulips. Or lilies."

He cocked his head. "Oh yeah?"

"Lilies represent humility, and tulips represent new beginnings, peace, and forgiveness," Hazel said.

He continued to rub the back of his neck, giving her a thoughtful look that made her very aware that her hair was in an unflattering ponytail and she hadn't reapplied her lipstick after lunch.

"You know your stuff when it comes to flowers," he said.

"You can't own a flower shop and not," she said.

"Good point. Tulips," he said. "Let's go with the tulips."

"Sure. Come with me." She led him to a different cooler. Was he staring at her ass as he followed her?

She reached into the cooler, pulling out a yellow and red tulip. "What do you think of these?"

He grinned, showing off that almost dimple again. "Red and yellow, huh?"

"Flame-like," she said. "Unless you actually did serious damage to the house, and then you might want to rethink giving them flowers the colour of flames."

"No real damage," he said. "I admire your restraint in not asking what happened. If I were you, I'd be grilling me for details."

"I am curious," she admitted.

He leaned a shoulder against the cooler, crossing his arms over his broad chest, a gorgeous male specimen in a fitted long-sleeved shirt and faded jeans that clung to his thick thighs. "I'm an electrician. My client asked me to look at their electrical panel because it was' glitchy' even though it was brand new. They failed to mention that they had installed the new one themselves and damaged some components. When I tried to remove the panel, the damaged components sparked, and the panel caught on fire."

"That doesn't sound like your fault," she said. "More like owner error."

He shrugged. "Client is still unhappy, and since I like working for myself and having food on the table, I'll take partial blame and bring tulips as a peace offering while I install their new electrical panel."

They studied each other. The cooler fan kicked in, a low buzz that drowned out the sound of Indie's voice as she spoke to the other customers. Was it Hazel's imagination, or was Hendrix seemingly obsessed with her mouth? He had to be at least six foot, which made her perfectly respectable 5'7", seem small. If he wanted to kiss her, he'd have to bend. Of course, she could make it easier for him by leaning in and standing on her tiptoes. Then he wouldn't need -

Hazel!

She realized with horror that she was doing just that. Leaning in and rising to her tiptoes. Her hand crushed the tulip's delicate stalk, and she took a step back, hoping it wasn't obvious what she'd been about to do.

Hendrix still leaned against the cooler, but his gaze had moved away from her mouth, and she could see red rising up his neck. The discomfort on his face made her want to cringe.

Shit. He knew. Hell, he could probably smell her need for him, even with the overwhelming scent of flowers and greenery.

Cursing herself for being such a fool, she said, "I can have the bouquet ready for tomorrow morning at nine."

"Perfect." He straightened and shoved his hands into his pockets, turning away before she could think of a way to apologize for attempting to make out with him in the middle of her store. "I'll drop by then."

"What's your budget?" she asked.

"No budget," he called over his shoulder as he walked toward the front. "Just whatever you think is," he waved a hand vaguely in the air, "best."

He was gone out the door, the bell jingling his exit before she could say anything else. She pressed her flaming forehead against the cooler door. She was a moron.

After only a few minutes, the bell jingled again, and then she heard Indie's footsteps as she approached.

"Your face is throwing off so much heat, you're making the cooler work overtime," Indie said. "C'mon, chin up, girl."

"Why? So you can tweeze my chin hairs for me?" Hazel didn't move.

8

Indie laughed and poked her in the ribs. "Tell me what happened with Mr. Tall, Dark, and Handsome."

"Nothing happened." Hazel straightened and stared at the crushed tulip in her hand. "His name is Hendrix, he's an electrician, he has an almost dimple, and I tried to kiss him."

Indie's mouth dropped open. "You what?"

The door opened, and two customers walked into the shop. Indie grabbed her wrist when Hazel walked by her. "You don't say something like that and then walk away, Hazel."

"Customers," Hazel said. "We'll talk about it later, okay?"

"Fine, but we are talking about it," Indie said before following her to the front.

CHAPTER 2

"Dad? Where are you?" The front door slammed, bringing with it a blast of cold air.

"In the kitchen," Hendrix called.

The heat kicked in with a low rumble, hot air blowing from the vent near his feet. It would snow soon. He needed to get his ass up to the cabin and do his final round of winterizing before the snow came.

"Hey." Preston walked into the kitchen, his jacket unbuttoned. and his head bare despite the cold. He wasn't wearing socks, either.

Hendrix resisted the urge to lecture him. His kid was twenty-three and well beyond the need for his dad to tell him how to dress appropriately for the weather. Old habits died hard, though. Preston had never been one to think about something as inconsequential as what he wore. His kid was a certified genius, and Hendrix couldn't be prouder of him, but being a genius came at a price. And for Preston, that price was an inability to focus on small details unrelated to molecular physics. Like dressing appropriately for the weather.

It's why Spencer was so good for him. Preston's

boyfriend was a born nurturer who didn't seem to mind Preston's inability to deal with small details. He also seemed to enjoy ensuring Preston ate three meals a day and didn't spend twenty-four/seven in his office at the university. Hendrix didn't think Spencer would ever truly understand how grateful he was to him.

"Hey, kid. How was your day?"

"Good. Yours? Set any more houses on fire?"

"Ha, ha." He lifted the lid from the slow cooker and stirred the stew. "You staying for dinner?"

"Nah, I'm meeting Spencer at his place in an hour. Just came by to see if you were still on for having dinner with Spencer's mom."

He stirred the stew again. "You finally convinced Spencer we should meet, huh?"

"Mostly," Preston said. "I'm still working on it, but I'm confident tonight's the night I'll convince him. It's stupid you haven't met her yet."

Preston ran a hand through his hair. He needed a haircut. Hendrix had no doubt that Spencer would have that taken care of in the next week or so. Honestly, he was surprised it had even got to this point.

"She's so great," Preston said. Like always, when the topic of Spencer's mother came up, Preston's entire demeanor changed. The only other time Hendrix saw his kid this animated was when he talked about atoms. "She had Spencer and me over for dinner the other night, and she just... she's really great."

Hendrix sat down across from Preston. Preston glomming onto Spencer's mother wasn't surprising. He was starved for a mother's affection. "I'm glad you like her, Preston."

"I do," Preston said. "I hate that Spencer wants to limit our time with her." He frowned. "She's not a bad person, and

12

I don't think she smothers him, but he's so big on this idea of being independent and not needing anyone. Everyone needs someone, Dad."

Hendrix smiled at him and tempered his urge to smooth down Preston's hair. His kid was sensitive. Sensitive and sweet and absentminded, and… perfect. "Yeah, they do."

"Anyway, Spencer likes you, you know? So, if you and his mom got along, maybe Spencer would think of it as more like four friends hanging out together rather than us hanging out with our parents."

Hendrix doubted it, but he kept his opinion to himself partly because he knew how difficult Preston found it to understand complex human emotions and partly because he didn't want to be the one to burst that bubble of hope in Preston's eyes and voice.

Thick, heavy guilt seeped into his chest. Still as sharp and painful as it was fifteen years ago when Preston's mother walked out on them. He knew it wasn't his fault, but knowing it had nothing to do with him didn't help the guilt. Hell, he wished it had been his fault. Wished it were some perceived flaw in him that Whitney hated instead of in their son.

"Shit, I gotta go." Preston stood.

Hendrix stood and wrapped him in a bear hug before he could wander away. "Love you, kid."

"Love you too." Preston returned his hug. "Thanks for agreeing to this."

"It's not a problem, but if Spencer doesn't want this, don't push too hard, okay? Spencer's relationship with his mom differs from ours, and you need to respect that."

"Yeah, I know," Preston said, but he was only half-listening. "It'll be good for him, though. She's nice, Dad. She's nice, and she's a great mom."

Hendrix's throat turned tight, and he pressed a rough kiss against the side of Preston's head. "She sounds great."

"You'll like her." Preston headed out of the kitchen and toward the front door. "She's kind of cute too. Maybe you'll hit it off with her."

He was gone in a blast of cold air before Hendrix could reply. He shook his head and returned to the counter, stirring the stew again before shutting off the slow cooker. He filled a bowl with stew, grabbed a spoon and a beer, and sat alone at the table.

He drank some of his beer. He hadn't dated anyone once Preston's mother left. He hadn't been a monk while raising Preston, but any... interactions with women had been one-offs and always when Preston was at physics camp or visiting his grandparents.

After Whitney left, he'd made a vow not to bring another woman into Preston's life, not willing to risk the chance that Preston would grow attached to them and then have his perfect, sensitive heart blown apart again.

Was it a mistake to do that? Preston's reaction to Spencer's mom, his obvious need and want for a mother, even at the age of twenty-three, suggested it might have been.

Hendrix ate a bite of stew, not tasting a thing as more guilt rolled through him. He'd thought he was doing the right thing by not letting anyone into his and Preston's life, by not allowing either of their hearts to be broken again, but where had that left them?

Preston craving a mother to the point of obsession, and Hendrix alone in a too big, too empty house night after night. Hell, he hadn't had sex with anything but his hand in over two years. At forty-eight years old, dating seemed too... difficult. He was too fucking old to be cruising the bars, and his solitary attempt at online dating had been a nightmare. Meeting women felt impossible.

You met someone today.

Heat prickled in his stomach, and his groin turned heavy. He reached down and adjusted himself before taking another swallow of beer. Hazel from the flower shop today had piqued his interest in a way that very few women had.

Her dark hair and dark eyes, the shape of her mouth, the curve of her ass in her jeans... he'd nearly sprouted wood right there in the shop. And that voice of hers... how would it sound when she moaned his name? Asked him to make her come? Begged him to fuck her?

Now he did get an erection, the pressure against the denim making him wince. He adjusted his dick again, but it did nothing to help. His attraction to Hazel was fierce and immediate, and he wasn't so thick-headed not to notice her attraction to him. He'd been close to kissing her in the middle of the damn shop, and he'd had to leave in a hurry before he'd done just that.

He would ask her out, he decided. When he picked up the flowers tomorrow, he would ask her to have dinner with him. The worst that could happen is she said no, right?

***

"I SWEAR, SIERRA, MY LIFE FLASHED BEFORE MY EYES." Indie sipped at her wine.

"Cork it, drama queen," Hazel said. "Yeah, the shelves in the back room are a little wobbly, but they were nowhere near about to tip over and crush you to death."

"You need to secure them to the wall," Indie said. "Seriously, honey. I have visions of you working late one night, the shelves collapsing, and you being trapped under those damn things."

"Not that I don't appreciate near-death stories," Sierra leaned forward, "but is that why you called an emergency meeting at Dawson's?" She glanced around the restaurant. "Also, how weird is it that Dawson's is our *place*, but we've never been here on a Sunday night? It feels different, right? Julia isn't even working."

Julia was their favourite server, and Hazel did have to admit that it felt weird to be here without her. "Do you think the fact that we have a favourite server means we spend too much time here?"

Sierra waved a perfectly manicured hand in the air. "Nothing wrong with weekly dinners at a restaurant with amazing food and the perfect, "she sipped at her drink, "whiskey sour."

"It's more than just once a week," Hazel said. "We were here three times last week."

Sierra shrugged. "I hate cooking. Anyway, why the emergency Sunday night dinner? What's going on?"

"Hazel met someone today," Indie said in a dramatic tone that made Hazel laugh.

"Oh my God, Indie, you make it sound like we're now dating and heading toward the altar."

"The only place you want to head to on him is south." Indie turned to Sierra. "I'm talking about his penis. She wants to go down on him. Get it?"

"I get it," Sierra said. "You're bad at euphemisms. You know that, right?"

"I mean, I'm not terrible at them," Indie said.

"Aren't you, though?" Sierra said.

Indie laughed. "The point is, Hazel met a very handsome man today, and she almost kissed him."

Sierra paused with her whiskey sour halfway to her mouth. "Come again?"

"If he's good with those big hands of his, she will be," Indie said.

Sierra laughed as Hazel rolled her eyes. "Don't be crude, Indie."

Indie just shrugged. Sierra stared pointedly at Hazel. "Spill it, babe."

"His name is Hendrix, he's an electrician with his own company, and I lost my mind and almost kissed him in the shop today when he was buying 'sorry I almost set your house on fire' tulips."

"So, he's good looking then?" Sierra said.

"You're not at all curious about the setting your house on fire thing?"

"Accidents happen," Sierra said. "I'm more curious about just how good looking this guy is if little Ms. 'I'm concentrating on my career and don't have time to fuck anyone' nearly kissed him right there in her flower shop."

Hazel turned beet red as their server, a young man with a shock of bright red hair and tattoos covering his forearms, slowly backed away. "I'll give you a few more minutes with the menus."

Indie burst into soft giggles when he practically sprinted to the safety of the other side of the restaurant. "Oh my God, his face. You just traumatized that poor kid, Sierra."

"Oh please, he's probably considering trying to hit on one of us. Women in their forties have crazy high sex drives, remember?" Sierra eyed their server like she might be considering taking him home.

"Sierra," Hazel said. "He's Michaela's age."

Sierra made a face. "Good point. Lusting after someone the same age as my kid is gross."

"If it had been Julia who overheard us, she wouldn't have blinked," Indie said with another laugh. "She probably would have sat down and joined in on the conversation. She's such a sweetheart."

"You know, for someone who hates the," Sierra made finger quotes, "Gen Z crowd, you sure love Julia."

"I don't hate them. I just find them super annoying and self-involved, and I am incredibly glad that I listened to what I genuinely wanted and didn't have kids. Even if it did cost me a husband."

Hazel squeezed her hand. "Adam was a dick for lying to you, Indie. He should have admitted from the very start that he wanted kids."

"Yeah," Indie said. "Anyway, Julia is different, and you know it. She reminds me of your kids." She smiled at Sierra and Hazel. "Who, until Julia came along, were the only Gen Z's I enjoyed spending time with."

"Anyway," Sierra said. "Back to Hazel almost kissing some random guy in the flower shop. How close were your lips to his?"

"Not that close," Hazel said. "But I did lean in and stood on my tiptoes like I wanted him to kiss me."

"What kind of flirting was he doing to invoke that kind of reaction?" Sierra said.

"That's the humiliating part," Hazel said. "He wasn't flirting. We were talking, and then I got weird, and he took off like his butt was on fire. I was so embarrassed I didn't make him fill out an order form or even ask him to prepay for his bouquet. I scared him."

Indie laughed. "Girl, you're so full of shit. You didn't scare him. He was into you. His eyes were glued to your ass when you led him to that second cooler."

"How do you know? You were with customers."

"I can do two things at once," Indie said. "You should ask him out when he picks up his flowers tomorrow."

"I can't," Hazel said.

"Why not?" Sierra said.

"Because if he were into me, he would have asked me out," Hazel said.

"Maybe he's shy. Ask him out," Sierra said. "The worst that can happen is he says no, right?"

"Right," Hazel said.

"Are you going to do it?" Indie said.

"Yes," Hazel said, taking a slug of her beer to hide her shock. Did she really agree to ask Hendrix the god out on a date?

"Good," Sierra said. "Text me and let me know how it goes."

"And me," Indie said. "I might not answer right away. I have two cat spays and a lump removal on a Burmese Mountain dog that's gonna be a bitch to take off, but I'll check my messages when I'm finished."

"Yeah, okay." Hazel took another swallow of beer. Her head buzzed, and it wasn't from the beer. What the hell was she doing?

CHAPTER 3

"Hey, Mom."

Hazel set down the knife and turned, leaning back against the counter. "Hi, honey. How are you?"

"Good." Spencer opened the fridge. "You mind if I make myself a sandwich? It was busy at the hospital today, and I didn't have time to grab lunch."

"Why don't you stay for supper," she said. "The chicken is almost done."

"Thanks, but I can't."

She resisted the urge to ask again. Her kid was the perfect split between her and his father. He was a nurturer like her, which partially made him such a good nurse, but he also had a pretty solid wall built around him, designed to keep everyone from seeing his true feelings.

Not everyone. Mostly just you.

She winced inwardly. It hurt so much because it was true, and she had no one to blame but herself. She'd tried too hard and overcompensated too much for her ex-husband's lack of interest in his own kid. Her over-interest, her desire to be the perfect mom to him, had backfired spectacularly. She'd annoyed Spencer and caused him to retreat.

She regretted it now, and after therapy and much self-reflection, she knew she was better at respecting Spencer's boundaries. But some days, especially hard days like this one, she wondered if she'd ever have the type of easy relationship with her son that she yearned for.

"Mom?"

She dragged herself out of painful reflections that didn't help her relationship with Spencer now. "Sorry, honey. What did you say?"

Spencer squirted mustard onto a slice of bread. "I asked why you're all dressed up today?"

"I'm not."

"Sure, you are. You're wearing make-up and a dress."

"I wear make-up every day." She turned and chopped more broccoli.

"Not like that." Spencer slapped the lunch meat between the bread and took a big bite. "You got a date or something?"

"No. How is Preston doing?"

"He's fine, still at the university. I'm picking him up at seven. He's going for a haircut, and then we'll grab something to eat."

"Tell him I said hi." She liked Spencer's boyfriend. Scratch that. She loved the kid. He was smart, funny, and just the tiniest bit awkward, and he was good for Spencer. Really good for him.

Is that why you like him? Or is it because it's obvious he likes you, and Spencer has been spending more time with you since he started dating Preston? There you go being selfish again and making it all about you, Hazel.

She shut down the negative self-talk before it could really

begin. It wasn't helpful, and besides, it wasn't true. Sure, she was grateful to Preston for encouraging Spencer to spend more time with her, but she liked him because Spencer was crazy about him, and it was apparent Preston was just as crazy about Spencer.

"I will." Spencer paused. "I'm asking him to move in with me."

She turned to face him again with a massive smile on her face. "Honey, that's wonderful. Congratulations."

"Thanks. We've been dating for a year, so I figure, you know, it's time. He's basically at my place ninety percent of the time anyway. It's a waste of money for him to rent his own place."

She laughed. "Maybe don't word it that way when you ask him to move in."

Spencer gave her a rare grin. "I'll make it romantic."

"Good," she said with another laugh. "Text me and tell me what he says."

Spencer scoffed. "Please, he'll text you himself. I know he texts you every day. Hell, you two have probably already discussed it."

"We haven't," Hazel said. While it was true that Preston texted her a lot, they rarely talked about Spencer beyond generalities. She didn't need a crystal ball to see that Preston was anxious for a mom. She didn't know the story behind Preston's mother. Although he'd mentioned his father a few times, he'd never once brought up his mother. She suspected that she'd died when Preston was a kid.

Afraid Spencer would think she was prying and trying to be too involved in his life again, she'd never asked him questions about any of Preston's family, even though she was intensely curious.

"Was work okay today?" Spencer still leaned against the

counter, those hazel eyes so much like his father's studying her intently.

"Fine, why?" She used a fork to poke at the potatoes that simmered on the stove.

"You seem... sad."

"I'm not," she said, infusing a cheeriness she didn't feel into her reply.

Even if she had a close relationship with Spencer, there was no way in hell she'd tell her kid she was depressed because she'd blown even the slimmest chance of banging the hottest guy she'd ever met. Spencer would run screaming from the house and never return. Then she really would be alone.

That thought sent fresh depression coursing through her. She shook it off. "I'm so happy for you, honey. Preston is a great guy."

"He is," Spencer said. "Do you have dinner plans for Thursday?"

"I don't," she said. "Do you and Preston want to come over for dinner? I can make lasagna. I know it's your favourite."

"Actually, I thought maybe you and me and Preston and his dad could have dinner together."

"Oh. Sure. I'd love to." She sounded casual enough but hoped her excitement didn't show on her face. She'd never met the family of Spencer's previous boyfriends. Not even Alex's family and Spencer had dated him for over a year.

"Cool. Preston's dad is a good cook, so we'll have dinner at his place. I'll text his address to you. Around seven?"

"Sure." And then, because she just couldn't help herself, she said, "I'm excited to meet him."

"It was Preston's idea," Spencer said quickly. "Hey, uh, act normal when you meet his dad, okay? He's a cool guy,

and I don't want him thinking that you're, like, weird and...
overbearing."

She held onto her smile with the grip of a rock climber
without a safety rope. "I'll do my best to be as cool as him."

"Right." Spencer's phone vibrated, and he snagged it
from his pocket. "I gotta go. I'll see you Thursday, okay?" He
leaned down and pecked her on the cheek. "Love you, Mom."

"Love you too, Spence."

She kept the smile glued to her face until she heard the
front door slam. The smile dropped from her face to shatter
on the floor, and she blinked back the hot tears. Christ, this
day was turning into an absolute shitshow.

She drained the potatoes and set to work mashing them,
adding sour cream, butter, and salt, before taking the chicken
out of the oven and placing it on a rack to cool while she
steamed the veggies. She'd made too much food. She always
did. Staring at a meal meant for a family rather than a single
divorcee only depressed her more.

She took the broccoli off the stove, left the potatoes in the
pot and the chicken cooling on the rack, and went upstairs.
Her appetite had disappeared, and she was suddenly
exhausted. She changed into her pajamas and went into the
bathroom to wash her face.

She studied herself in the mirror above the sink. She was
wearing more make-up than normal and had, in fact, spent
closer to half an hour this morning than her usual ten minutes
doing her make-up.

It had been for nothing. Hendrix hadn't picked up the
flowers this morning. Instead, a young Black man in a blue
golf shirt with "Smith's Electrical Ltd." on the front pocket
had picked up the tulips.

She washed her face, smoothed on some face cream, and
returned downstairs. She'd spent a few minutes at lunch

shamelessly googling Hendrix's company. The company had a basic website and a Facebook page, but either his personal Facebook page was set entirely to private, or he never posted to it. He didn't even have a picture for his profile.

She started carving the chicken, even though her appetite hadn't re-appeared. So, the slim chance that she might go on a date with a hot guy hadn't worked out. No big deal. If she was so anxious to have sex, she could try online dating again.

She shuddered on reflex. She'd known plenty of people who'd done well with online dating, hell, her book club was rife with them, but it hadn't worked for her. The few men she'd gone on dates with had only been interested in sex, and while she missed sex, *craved* sex with something other than her damn vibrator, she also wanted more.

Still, it was dumb to be so depressed over never seeing Hendrix again. Hell, even if she hadn't weirded him out so much that he was forced to send someone else to pick up the flowers, there was no guarantee he'd have even said yes to a date.

She needed to forget about him.

HENDRIX WAS NERVOUS, WHICH WAS STUPID BECAUSE, AT HIS age, asking a woman out for dinner shouldn't make his back sweat and his palms itch.

Still, his back *was* sweating, and his palms *were* itchy. Hendrix wiped his hands on his jeans and slid out of his work truck. The work emergency yesterday morning that stopped him from picking up the flowers put him in a fuck of a mood for the rest of the day. So much so that Jacob had finally asked him what bee had flown up his ass. Considering his apprentice barely said two sentences in a day, it was a testament to how much of a dick Hendrix was being.

He'd apologized to Jacob and even managed to refrain all goddamn day from asking if the gorgeous flower shop owner had happened to ask about Hendrix when Jacob picked up the flowers.

He'd spent most of today impatient to return to the flower shop and daydreaming about how Hazel's breasts might look in his hands. He was lucky he hadn't electrocuted himself.

He slammed his door shut and straightened his shirt before crossing the street to the Flower Pot. He stepped inside, looking around eagerly for Hazel. A young Latino man wearing a green apron over a blue top and an ankle-length, flowered skirt smiled at him from near the glass counter.

"Hi, welcome to the Flower Pot."

"Thanks," Hendrix said.

He scanned the store. There was no sign of Hazel. Maybe she'd already left. It was Tuesday evening and the store closed in half an hour.

"Are you shopping for a specific occasion?" The sales clerk joined him. The tag on his apron said his name was Carlos. He was young, nineteen or twenty maybe, with an open and cheerful face.

"Actually, I'm wondering if Hazel was in today?"

Carlos nodded. "Yeah, she's in the back. Give her five minutes, and she'll be -"

The terrific crash coming from the back of the store made Carlos sprint past the coolers, and the swinging door marked employees only. Hendrix didn't hesitate. He followed Carlos, pushing through the swinging door and stopping behind him.

"Holy shit!" Carlos stared at the explosion of floral supplies on the floor.

Hendrix moved past him, navigating the floral tape and wire, floral foam, clear containers, hundreds of spools of ribbons, and the rolls of cellophane, tissue, and wrapping paper that littered the floor.

He stepped over the floor-to-ceiling wooden shelf that was lying face down on the floor. Hazel stood in the middle of the mess, her eyes wide and a look of slack shock on her face. Her shoulder-length dark hair was in a messy bun on top of her head, and she wore a t-shirt and jeans under her Flower Pot apron.

Hendrix cupped her face, his other hand smoothing down her arm. "Hazel, are you hurt?"

She blinked up at him. "I... Hendrix? What are you doing here?"

"Are you hurt?" he repeated as he scanned her up and down. "Did the shelf fall on you?"

"No. I – it fell over, but it didn't hit me. I was standing, and it just fell around me, kind of over me..." she gestured vaguely at the shelf.

He blew out his breath in relief. Luckily, Hazel had been standing in a spot where, when the shelf tipped over, the space between the third and fourth shelf had passed right over her rather than one of the actual shelves smashing into her.

"You sure?" he said, even though he could see she wasn't hurt. He rubbed his thumb over her cheekbone. "The shelf didn't hit you?"

"No." She stared at him, her dark eyes still full of shock. "I'm okay."

"Oh man, what a mess," Carlos said.

Hazel blinked and stepped back, withdrawing from his touch before staring at the floor. "Indie was right. She said the shelves would tip over, and I told her they wouldn't."

"At least it wasn't the shelves with the vases and shit."

Carlos pointed to the second floor-to-ceiling shelf. "Can you imagine how much broken glass there'd be?"

Hendrix reached out and touched the shelf with vases, baskets, water tubes, bottles of bleach, more floral foam, and boxes of raffia and pins. It wobbled even under his light touch, and he muttered a curse. "This is an accident waiting to happen. You need to secure the shelves to the wall."

"Hey, thanks, Captain Obvious."

He turned to study Carlos, who gave him a light-hearted smile. "Sorry, man, but you deserved that."

"Fair enough," Hendrix said with a grin.

The bell over the front door jingled, and Hazel rubbed at her forehead. "Carlos, can you go back up front? I'll start cleaning this up."

"Sure. Listen, I can stay after we're closed and help you clean up," Carlos said.

"Thanks, honey, I appreciate that," Hazel said.

Carlos turned and pushed through the swinging door.

"He seems like a good kid," Hendrix said.

"They," Hazel said absently as she bent and picked up a box of wire. "Carlos uses they/them pronouns."

"Right," Hendrix said.

She stared silently at him for a minute. "If you're here to tell me the tulip bouquet was terrible, this is so not the moment."

He laughed. "The flowers were perfect, and my client appreciated the gesture."

"Good." She swiped at her forehead. "So, uh, why are you here?"

Now didn't seem like the right time to ask her for dinner. Instead, he said, "How about I help you pick up this shelf?"

"Oh no, that's okay," Hazel said. "We can do it."

"Unless Carlos is stronger than they look, you'll need my help," he said.

"They're pretty wiry," she said with a small smile.

"Let me help," he said. "I can grab my tools from my truck and anchor the shelf to the wall before you pile all the supplies on it again."

"I thought you were an electrician," she said.

"I am," Hendrix said. "But before I got my electrician's certificate, I worked as a general labourer. I can still swing a hammer and use a screwdriver like a boss."

She laughed, and his groin tightened in response. Fuck, she was beautiful.

"Well, if you're sure," she said.

"Positive," he said. "I'll get my tools."

"Thank you, Hendrix."

"You're welcome, Hazel."

CHAPTER 4

"I t's true." Carlos stuffed the last bite of pizza into their mouth. "The guy ordered seventeen bouquets of a dozen roses each."

"That's a lot of roses," Hendrix said.

"Right?" Carlos shook their head. "I thought maybe it was for an anniversary, been married seventeen years, that kind of shit, yeah?"

Hendrix nodded and reached for the final slice of pizza in the box. He hesitated with his hand hovering above it, glancing at Hazel. "Did you want the last slice?"

"Go ahead," she said.

He took the slice, curled it sideways and took a big bite of the end. Was it weird that she liked watching him eat? It was weird, right?

"So, it wasn't for an anniversary?" Hendrix said to Carlos when he'd finished chewing.

Carlos shook their head. "No. Get this - the guy had them delivered to seventeen different women."

"You're kidding." Hendrix paused with his slice halfway to his mouth.

"I'm not," Carlos said. "The dude had seventeen side pieces."

"That's a lot to keep track of," Hendrix said solemnly.

Hazel laughed, and he grinned at her, making that almost but not quite a dimple appear in his cheek.

"You're telling me," Carlos said. "Also, the stamina, right? I mean, he had to be guzzling Gatorade on the regular, yeah? His electrolytes would have been real low."

Hendrix laughed hard. Carlos shrugged. "You know I'm right. Screwing that many women... you gotta keep your electrolytes up."

They glanced at Hazel. "Shit. Sorry, Hazel. That's crude talk for at work."

"Considering you stayed nearly three extra hours and helped clean up one hell of a mess, a little crudeness is forgivable," Hazel said.

"It looks a lot better. And safer," Carlos glanced at the shelf.

After the shop closed, the three of them picked up the shelf, and Hendrix secured the shelf to the wall before sticking around to help her and Carlos clean up. The shelf was now a beautiful, organized display of floral supplies. Considering how messy it had been before, it was almost a blessing that the whole thing had come crashing down on her.

"Once you have the other shelf cleaned off, I'll stop by and secure it to the wall as well," Hendrix said.

"I appreciate that," Hazel said. "I'll come in early on Sunday and remove all the stuff, but whatever day and time works for you would be fine."

"Sunday will work," Hendrix said. "What time does the shop open on Sunday?"

"Ten," Hazel said.

"I could come by around nine," he said.

"Perfect." She brushed pizza crumbs from her jeans and reminded herself it wasn't a date.

Carlos glanced at their phone and slid off the stool. "I better go. I told Derek I'd meet him at nine." They paused before turning to Hazel. "I'll wait and walk you to your car."

She smiled at Carlos. "Thanks, honey, but that's not necessary. I'll be fine."

Carlos glanced at Hendrix, who said, "I'll walk her to her car."

"Thanks." Carlos held out their fist, and Hendrix bumped it.

Hazel wanted to be irritated but found it difficult. She could take care of herself, she'd taken several self-defense courses over the last couple of years, but there was something oddly appealing about Hendrix being worried for her safety.

"Bye, Hazel. I'll see you tomorrow." Carlos had already grabbed their jacket and backpack. "Thanks for the pizza."

"Thank you for staying, Carlos. I really appreciate it," Hazel said.

"Anytime." They waved to Hendrix. "Nice to meet you, man."

"You too," Hendrix said.

Hazel followed Carlos to the front of the shop, leaving Hendrix in the back room. "Have a good night, honey."

"You too." Carlos's grin was wicked. "Don't do anything with Hendrix that I would do."

She laughed. "Good night, Carlos."

"Night, Hazel."

She locked the door behind them and returned to the back of the store. Hendrix had gathered up the empty pizza box and their used napkins and put them in the large garbage can next to the back door. Their empty soda cans were placed neatly in the recycling bin.

"Thank you," she said.

"You bet." He shoved his hands into his pockets. "Do you need to cash out before you go?"

She shook her head. "I'll come in early tomorrow. I'm ready to call it a day."

He waited patiently as she gathered her things before walking to the front door with her. She set the alarm, and they stepped outside. He shifted his toolbox to the other hand as she locked the door. She could see a truck with a 'Smith's Electrical' logo plastered to the door parked across the street.

She smiled at him. "I'm parked around back in the lot."

"All right," he said.

"You don't have to walk me to my actual car," she said. "It's not that late, and I can take care of myself."

"Are you trying to put me on Carlos's bad side?" Hendrix said.

She laughed. "No, but I've taken some self-defense courses, so…."

"So, you could kick my ass, is what you're saying?"

She shrugged with a smug smile on her face, and he laughed. "Humour me then and let me walk you to your car so I can feel manly and strong. What do you say?"

"Sure," she said, "but if we get mugged, it's every man for themselves."

"Harsh but fair," Hendrix said.

They walked half a block to the alley before heading down it. She was very aware of the hard warmth of Hendrix's big body next to hers. The darkness of the alley had her considering manufacturing a pretend trip just as an excuse to grab his hand. She rolled her eyes at herself. She wasn't a teenager, for God's sake.

"It's a beautiful night," she said as they breached the mouth of the alley and stepped into the parking lot.

"It is," he said.

"Cold," she said. "It'll probably snow soon."

Oh my God, Hazel. You're talking about the weather? The weather?

She cringed inwardly. Her decision to ask Hendrix out for dinner poked at the back of her brain, but now that the time had come, it was much easier to make boring small talk about the weather.

She stopped at her car. "Well, this is me." She opened the door and threw her purse into the passenger seat. "Thank you again for staying to help clean up and for securing the shelf. I really appreciate it."

"No problem."

She cleared her throat. "Right. So, um..."

Just ask, Hazel!

He stared down at her, those pretty blue eyes of his unreadable in the dim glow of the streetlights.

"I was wondering if...."

"What?" he asked.

She couldn't do this. At least not now. She would ask him on Sunday when she was wearing more makeup and a pretty dress and could formulate a more solid plan of asking.

"Nothing," she said. "Good night, Hendrix."

Coward.

He set down his toolbox and caught her hand before she could slide into the car. "Hazel, would you like to have dinner with me?"

"Yes," she said, her pulse going haywire. "Yes, I would."

He smiled, his hand tightening a little on hers. "Friday?"

"Friday works. I should be finished work by six."

"I know a great restaurant not too far from here. I could pick you up from the store at six if you're comfortable with that?"

"I am," she said.

"Okay."

"I'll see you Friday at six," she said.

"Yes." He still held her hand. She shivered all over when he stared down at their clasped hands and then ran his thumb over the pulse point in her wrist.

His gaze lifted to her face and narrowed in on her mouth. When he bent, she stood on her tiptoes and leaned in. His warm breath grazed her cheek, and then his mouth brushed hers.

His lips were warm and firm and perfect. He kissed her again, and she returned the kiss, her cheeks flushing with warmth and desire starting a slow beat in her belly. She parted her lips, hoping he would take the hint. His tongue touched her bottom lip. She was a little embarrassed by her soft moan, but the sound seemed to encourage him. His arm slid around her waist, tugging her forward until she was pressed against his hard body.

He deepened the kiss, sliding his tongue into her mouth to explore and tease. They kissed hungrily, exploring each other's mouths with undisguised enthusiasm. He released her mouth and let her take in a single breath before he kissed her again.

Hendrix's big hand squeezed her hip. She pressed her pelvis against him. That delicious hardness she could feel against her stomach made her pussy clench and her clit throb.

Would he think her too forward if she dragged him into the back seat of her car and rode him like a pony? She was willing to take the chance that he might. Before she could make the suggestion, Hendrix pulled away.

She stared up at him, her body shuddering with need. "Hendrix?"

"Sorry," he said hoarsely. He reached down and pulled at

the front of his jeans. The obvious bulge made her mouth water. "You should go, Hazel."

Embarrassment blotted out the desire, and her cheeks flamed red. Hendrix cursed and grabbed her hand. "That came out wrong. I mean that I have no control when I'm around you. You should go before I try to convince you to fuck me in the back seat of your car."

She stared mutely at him, fresh desire slamming into her. His nostrils flared before he muttered another curse. "Jesus, Hazel, do not look at me like that."

He pulled her close again and pressed a hard, almost bruising kiss against her mouth. "As much as I would love to fuck you right here and now, I'm too old to be arrested for indecent exposure."

She laughed jaggedly as he rested his forehead against hers. "Me too."

He sucked in a deep breath. "At least we know there's chemistry, right?"

Another jagged laugh. "Yeah."

He kissed her forehead. "I'll see you Friday, okay?"

She nodded. "Okay. Good night, Hendrix."

"Night, Hazel." He stepped back reluctantly. She stared at him, wondering what he would think if she invited him back to her house. She was tempted. So, fucking tempted. But she wasn't looking for just sex. She was looking for a relationship, and if she invited him home, if she took him to her bed and did all the dirty, delicious things she wanted to do to him, the odds of her never seeing him again was extremely high.

He isn't that kind of guy.

Maybe. Maybe not. She didn't know him all that well.

"You all right?" he asked.

"Yes." Away from the heat of his body, the cold air had

seeped in through her jacket. Her cheeks were numb, and her teeth chattered.

Hendrix took her hand and squeezed it. "Go home before you freeze to death, Hazel. I'll see you on Friday."

"Okay. Bye, Hendrix."

"Bye, Hazel." He brushed an entirely too chaste kiss against her cheek.

She climbed into her car and started it, cranking the heat to high before she waved at Hendrix and backed out of her stall. With one final glance at him in the rear-view mirror, she drove away.

CHAPTER 5

"I t smells delicious, Dad."

"Thanks, kid." Hendrix stirred the gravy that simmered on the back burner. "Can you grab the package of buns out of the pantry and put them in that basket?"

"What? You didn't make fresh buns from scratch?" Preston said in mock horror. "We're trying to make a good impression, Dad."

"Just the fact that you can cook will impress her." Spencer reached into the pantry for the package of buns. "My dad doesn't even know how to boil an egg. He was super critical of my mom's cooking, though."

"Your dad's a dick," Preston said.

"Preston," Hendrix said.

"What? He is. I've met him. He spent the entire dinner talking about himself and didn't even ask Spencer about his job or what was going on in his life."

Hendrix looked at Spencer, who shrugged. "He is kind of selfish."

Preston glanced at the clock on the wall. "I wonder where your mom is. She should be here by now."

"She texted me. She's running a little late because she had a last-minute customer at the store," Spencer said.

Hendrix stirred the whipped potatoes and tasted them before adding more salt and butter. Spencer rarely spoke about his mother, but he'd mentioned she worked in retail without giving any other details. Preston hadn't told him anything else either. When it came to Spencer's mom, Preston focused only on what made her a great mom. The small details, like what she did for a living, weren't something he ever brought up. Again, not surprising, but Hendrix realized he didn't even know the woman's first name.

"Mr. Smith, don't worry about trying to impress my mom, okay?" Spencer said. "My mom is -"

"She's great," Preston said. "You're too hard on her, Spence. God."

"You didn't grow up with her. She doesn't understand the concept of personal space," Spencer said.

Preston frowned. "You keep saying that, but I don't see it. She never comes by your place without checking if it's okay first. She doesn't, like, pry into your personal life when we have dinner with her, and my dad texts me more often than she texts you."

Spencer shrugged again. "It's true that she's much better than she used to be, but she's not cool like your dad."

"One, my dad isn't cool -"

"Hey," Hendrix said, "I'm cool."

Preston grinned at him before saying, "And two, parents aren't supposed to be cool anyway."

Spencer's phone buzzed. "She's here."

"Tell her she can park in the driveway," Hendrix said as Preston and Spencer headed out of the kitchen.

He'd parked his work truck in the garage with the SUV so

there would be room for both Spencer's car and his mother's car in the driveway. He removed the tin foil from the roast and grabbed the carving knife. He'd made too much food, even for the four of them, but he'd send the leftovers home with Preston and Spencer. He wouldn't need them, not with his date tomorrow night and then hopefully...

He cleared his throat and sliced off a piece of roast. Thinking that he might convince Hazel to not only sleep with him Friday night but allow him to spend the entire weekend with her was madness. One, she had to work, and two, just because they had crazy intense chemistry didn't mean she would sleep with him immediately. It hadn't stopped him from indulging in some fantasies for the last few days, though. Ones that primarily involved his face buried between Hazel's smooth thighs or her riding him with those amazing tits bouncing and her sexy voice begging him to give it to her harder.

He'd get an erection if he kept thinking this way. Sporting a woody the first time he met Spencer's mother wasn't the impression he wanted to make. He tried to clear his mind of images of Hazel as he sliced up the roast beef.

The front door slammed, and when he heard their footsteps coming down the hall, he put a smile on his face and turned around.

"Mr. Smith, I'd like you to meet my mom -"

"Hazel?" He stared in wide-eyed shock at Hazel. Her dark hair was down and brushing against her shoulders, and her lips were shiny with gloss. She wore a green dress that accentuated her perfect breasts and the curve of her hips. "What are you... you're Spencer's mom?"

The surprise on her face matched his, and her hand clenched on the wine bottle she held. "Hendrix?"

"You guys know each other?" Preston asked.

Hazel glanced at Spencer. Confusion covered his face, and a weird flicker of regret crossed hers before she turned to Preston. "Your dad came into my shop the other day to buy some flowers."

"Cool," Preston said. "For the clients whose house you tried to burn down?"

"A small fire that didn't move past the electrical box," Hendrix said. "But yes, for those clients."

Preston laughed and put his arm around Spencer's waist. "Small world, huh, Spencer?"

Spencer nodded, but he was gnawing at his bottom lip and giving Hazel a suspicious look. "Are you guys, like, friends or something? Why do you know each other's names?"

"Oh my God, are you the guy who helped Hazel secure the shelf to the wall when it fell on her?" Preston asked.

"Shelf? What shelf?" Spencer said.

"The one in the shop's back room," Preston said. "The wobbly one. It came crashing down Sunday night. She didn't tell you?"

Spencer shook his head and turned to his mom. "The shelf fell on you?"

"No, no," Hazel said. "It fell around me."

"Were you hurt?" Spencer asked.

"No, not at all. It just made a huge mess. Hendrix, uh, Mr. Smith, happened to be in the store at the time, and he offered to secure the shelf to the wall for me."

"That's hilarious that it was my dad," Preston said. "What are the odds?"

Spencer still gave his mother a weirdly suspicious look. "So, you didn't know he was Preston's dad?"

"No," Hazel said. "I swear, Spencer."

"What's the big deal?" Preston said. "So, they've met

before, and he helped her at the store. What's wrong, Spencer?"

"Nothing," Spencer said. "It isn't a big deal." His face suggested it was, though, and Hazel looked positively sick to her stomach.

Her face pale except for two red spots high on her cheeks, she gave Hendrix a spectacularly unnatural smile and held out the wine bottle. "I brought some wine. I wasn't sure what was on the menu, so I chose white. I hope that's okay."

"It's perfect. Thank you," he said as he took the wine from her.

There was an awkward silence. Hazel rubbed her hands compulsively against her hips, and Spencer continued to give her a distrustful look that Hendrix didn't understand. "Preston, why don't you pour Hazel a glass of wine."

"Sure," Preston said.

"Do you need help with dinner?" Hazel said.

"We're good, just finishing up. You sit and relax," Hendrix said. "How was work today?"

"Oh, um, good. Lots of customers today." She cleared her throat as she sat down and smiled at Spencer. "How did your shift go last night?"

"Fine. Busy." Spencer put the buns in the basket on the table and sat beside her. "Mr. Angston finally went home."

"That's great news," Hazel said.

"His wife gave me a card and a Starbucks gift card. She said she was happy I was his nurse and appreciated everything I'd done for him."

"I'm not surprised," Hazel said. "You're amazing at your job."

"He really is." Preston bent and gave Spencer a quick kiss before handing the glass of wine to Hazel.

"Thank you, Preston." Hazel sipped at the wine. "How did your meeting with the university president go?"

"Nothing to worry about." Preston sat down beside her.

Hendrix paused in carving the roast. "You had a meeting with the president?"

"Yeah, but it was nothing. Just wanted to talk about some event I'm supposed to attend at the university." He waved his hand carelessly. "I don't want to go, but Spencer is making me."

Spencer laughed. "You have to go, honey. It's required. Besides, how often do I get to see you in a tux?"

Hazel took another sip of wine. Even from his spot at the counter, Hendrix could see she was still weirdly tense. He set the platter of meat on the table before bringing over the potatoes and the roasted vegetables.

"It looks delicious, Mr. Smith," Hazel said.

He studied her for a moment. "Call me Hendrix."

"Sure, okay," she said with a peek at Spencer.

Preston had poured all of them a glass of wine, and Hendrix took a sip from the glass in front of him. "Thank you again for bringing wine."

"My pleasure." Her small and formal smile looked like it hurt to produce.

"Dig in before it gets cold," Hendrix said and handed the potatoes to Preston.

HENDRIX LOADED THE LAST OF THE DISHES INTO THE dishwasher before scrubbing at the pots soaking in the sink. If it hadn't been for Preston, dinner would have been excruciatingly uncomfortable. Seemingly oblivious to Hazel's discomfort and the tenseness radiating from Spencer, he'd kept up a steady stream of chatter, mostly directed at Hazel. It was evident that Preston not only liked Hazel but loved her, and Hendrix hoped like hell it didn't go horribly wrong.

He scrubbed at some dried potatoes on the inside of the pot. He'd have to speak with Hazel on Friday night, give her a heads up about Preston's past with his mother, and hopefully help her understand why Preston had imprinted on her like a baby bird.

Not that she seemed to mind. Even with her obvious discomfort, she'd been kind to Preston and seemed genuinely interested in everything he had to say. At twenty-three, Preston still seemed almost painfully young in some ways. Once they finished dinner, he'd wanted to show Hazel his childhood bedroom, which was exactly how he'd left it when he moved out. Hendrix planned to turn it into a home gym, but every time he'd brought it up, he didn't need to be a genius to see that it upset Preston. He'd left it as it was. If Preston needed the comfort of his childhood room for a few years longer, Hendrix was okay with that.

He checked the microwave clock. The three of them had been upstairs for close to fifteen minutes. Hendrix smiled a little. No doubt, Preston was showing her all the awards he'd won throughout high school.

"Hendrix?"

He turned, his pulse accelerating at just the sight of Hazel standing in the doorway. "Hey there."

"Hi." She rubbed at her hips again. "The boys are still upstairs. They got caught up in looking at Preston's old yearbooks. I can't believe he graduated high school when he was fifteen. I mean, I can because he told me and showed me his graduation pictures, but still... your kid is a genius."

"He is," Hendrix said. "I had him tested and everything."

That earned him a small smile but not the laugh he had hoped for.

"Preston is a terrific kid," she said. "I like him a lot."

"So is Spencer," Hendrix said. "He's great for Preston, and I'm happy they're a couple."

"Did you know they're moving in together?" she said.

"Yeah, Preston texted me the day Spencer asked him to move in. I'm in charge of helping load the U-haul."

"They have a move-in date already?"

"Yeah, next weekend. You didn't know?"

"Spencer hadn't mentioned it to me," she said.

She hesitated and then moved toward him, grabbing the dishtowel off the counter. "I can dry the pots."

He scrubbed at the pot. "So, quite the coincidence, huh?"

"Yes. Very small world," she said.

He rinsed the pot and handed it to her before starting on the next.

"Thank you for dinner," she said. "It was delicious, and you're a great cook."

"Thanks. I'm glad you could join us."

She dried the pots with quick, efficient swipes of the dishtowel. Her body was tense, and he could see a muscle twitching in her temple.

"I'm looking forward to tomorrow night," he said.

"About that," she said, "I'm afraid I have to cancel."

"Okay," he said as hot disappointment bubbled in his guts. "What about Saturday night instead?"

She glanced at the doorway. "Um, I can't... I mean... I don't think we should date."

He paused with his hands in the water. "Did I do something wrong?"

"No, no," she said. Her hand fluttered out like she was

going to touch him before she thought better of it and gripped the towel again. "It's not you. It's me."

He made a face, and she grimaced. "Jesus, that's so cliché."

"It really is," he said.

She sighed. "It's complicated, okay?"

"It doesn't have to be."

"Look," she made another nervous peek at the doorway, "Spencer would hate it if I dated you and -"

"You're an adult, and so is your kid," he said. "Is your dating life any of his business?"

"I told you it was complicated. I don't have the best relationship with Spencer, and I've been working hard to fix it. If I date you, it'll ruin every bit of progress I've made with him."

"What do you mean?"

She shook her head. "It would take way too long to explain. I like you, Hendrix, but we can't date. I'm sorry."

"What if I spoke to Spencer?"

"No!" Now she had a death grip on the dishtowel. She stepped closer and dropped her hand on his arm, squeezing urgently. "Do not speak to Spencer about this, Hendrix. I'm serious. You can't mention that we," her gaze dropped to his mouth for a few seconds, "kissed or anything like that. Okay?"

Before he could reply, Preston and Spencer walked into the kitchen. Spencer stared at Hazel's hand on his arm. "Mom? What are you doing?"

"Nothing." Hazel let go of his arm, the guilty look of a woman on death row plastered all over her face. "Just saying thank you to Mr. Smith for dinner."

Preston grabbed a soda from the fridge, oblivious to the

tension in the room. "Hey, I thought maybe the four of us could play cribbage. What do you think, Dad?"

"Sure," Hendrix said. "The board's in my office, I think."

"Do you like card games, Hazel?" Preston asked.

Before she could reply, Spencer said, "Mom has to get going, honey."

"What? Why?" Preston said.

"It's getting pretty late," Spencer said, "and she likes to go to bed early."

"Dude, it's, like, nine o'clock," Preston said. "Besides, your mom is a night owl. I text her after eleven all the time. What do you say, Hazel? One game of crib?"

"She can't," Spencer said. "Right, Mom?"

He stared pointedly at Hazel, who nodded and said, "I have some bookkeeping for the shop to finish."

"Oh, c'mon, just one game," Preston said. "Dad loves crib and hardly ever gets to play. Isn't that right, Dad?"

"Yes," Hendrix said.

"Maybe next time, honey." Hazel held out her hand to Hendrix. "Thank you again for dinner, Mr. Smith. I enjoyed it, and it was so nice to formally meet you."

"You as well." He shook her hand, hating how it trembled in his grip.

Hazel hugged Preston and kissed his cheek. "Have a great weekend, Preston."

"Yeah." Preston looked like he'd lost the championship round of *Jeopardy*. "I'll text you tomorrow, okay?"

"Sure." She smiled at him before hugging Spencer. "Bye, honey. Love you."

"I'll walk you to your car." Spencer smiled at Preston. "Grab the crib board and get it set up. I won't be long."

The smile on Hazel's face dropped for only a second before it cemented back into place. Still, Hendrix felt her hurt as keenly as if it had crushed him like a tidal wave. How could Spencer be so obtuse about his mother's feelings?

"Enjoy your game," she said to Preston and gave Hendrix a little wave without actually looking at him.

She and Spencer left. Preston waited until he heard the front door close before grinning at Hendrix. "Well, what do you think? She's great, right?"

"She is," Hendrix said.

Preston opened his soda and took a long drink. "So, you'd be open to the idea of the four of us hanging out?"

"Sure," he said. "But do you think that's something Spencer wants?"

Preston shrugged. "It's good for him. He has this idea of who his mom is, which is completely wrong. I don't get it."

"Maybe she's different with him."

"I don't think so. He's so fixated on how she was when he was a teenager, that he can't just relax and give her a chance. You know? He makes it hard when it doesn't have to be."

"Relationships are complicated," Hendrix said. "Don't push Spencer too hard, okay, kid? I know you want him to be happy and have a good relationship with his mom, but Spencer needs to want that too."

"I know." Preston drank some more soda. "It's why I think the four of us hanging out would be good. Maybe he'll see another side of his mom if he sees her with people her age."

Hendrix had to tamp down on his smile. God, he loved this kid. "Well, I'm open to the four of us having dinner or whatever, but if Spencer or Hazel isn't, don't push them for it. Okay?"

"I won't push hard," Preston said. "But I'm gonna try. Hazel is awesome, and she deserves to have her kid see that. Don't you agree?"

"Yes," he said.

"Cool. I'm gonna get the crib board. Be right back."

Preston left, and Hendrix leaned against the counter. He was all for spending more time with Hazel. Despite her refusal to date him, the idea of being with her was still intoxicating, but he was confident Preston would find it more difficult than he thought to get Spencer and Hazel to agree to it.

CHAPTER 6

Hazel lugged another box of vases from the shelf and set it on the floor. She had one shelf left to clear off and then she could anchor the shelving unit to the wall. She wiped the sweat from her forehead and sipped at her coffee.

She stared doubtfully at the drill she'd borrowed from Sierra. Using power tools was not her strength, but after what happened with the other shelving unit, she needed to anchor this one. And it wasn't like she could expect Hendrix to show up. Not after how cold she was to him on Thursday night.

She muttered a curse and leaned against the other shelf, rubbing the spot between her eyebrows. It had to be just her fucking luck that Hendrix was Preston's dad. What were the odds that the first guy she was interested in, in a very long time, would be off-limits?

It wasn't fair. She deserved to be happy, right?

At the expense of your relationship with Spencer?

She stared at the coffee cup in her hand, her stomach churning a mixture of bitter coffee and bile. No, not at the expense of her relationship with Spencer. She'd made many mistakes as a mom when Spencer was growing up. She now had a second chance, and she wouldn't fuck it up, even for a hot guy.

Especially not for a hot guy. What kind of mom did it make her if she gave up on her relationship with her kid just so she could get laid?

A shitty one.

She cocked her head, frowning as she straightened and stared at the swinging door. She could have sworn she heard someone knocking on the front door. She glanced at her watch when she heard knocking again. It was only nine, and the shop didn't open until ten. Maybe she or Carlos had left the sign flipped to open last night?

She hesitated, tempted beyond belief to stay where she was and let the customer figure it out. With a soft sigh, she set her coffee cup on the shelf and headed toward the front. Her little shop was doing well, but every customer counted. It wouldn't kill her to open a little early.

She stopped next to the counter, staring wide-eyed at Hendrix standing outside on the sidewalk. He held a toolbox in one hand and raised an eyebrow at her, his voice muffled by the glass. "You gonna open the door?"

Her heart racing, she hurried forward and opened the door, standing back to give Hendrix room to step inside before she locked the door again. "Hendrix, what... um, what are you doing here?"

"I'm here to anchor the shelf to the wall." He set his toolbox down and blew on his hands. "Christ, it's cold out there this morning."

When she just stared blankly at him, he said, "What? We said Sunday morning around nine, right?"

"Yes, but..."

"But what?" he said.

"I didn't think you would still help me after I broke off our date."

He studied her silently before shrugging. "I guess you don't know me very well yet."

"Yet?" she said.

He shrugged again. "Our kids are dating, Hazel. We'll have to spend some time together."

"No, I know," she said. "I just, I want to be clear that we can't -"

"Date. I remember." He picked up his toolbox. "Is that coffee I smell?"

She nodded. "I have a Keurig in the back. Do you want a cup?"

"I would love one," he said.

He followed her to the back of the store. She wished she had worn something other than her usual jeans and a t-shirt, but she hadn't expected Hendrix to show up.

She led him to the coffee machine, and he made himself a cup of coffee, grabbing some creamer from the mini fridge and adding a surprisingly large amount of sugar.

"You like it sweet, huh?" she said.

His gaze dipped to her mouth. "I do."

Her temptation to fuck him right there in the back room was highly distracting. She walked over to the wobbly shelf. "So, I have the one shelf left to clear off, and then it's ready. Give me five minutes."

"I can help," he said.

"No, no, drink your coffee." She tugged self-consciously at her t-shirt before beginning to clear off the shelf. "How is your weekend going?"

"Fine," he said. "Watched the football game yesterday with a friend, and this afternoon I'm helping Preston and

Spencer take apart their entertainment center, so it's easier to load into the U-Haul this weekend."

She heaved another box of heavy vases onto the floor before smiling at him. "It's so nice of you to help them with the moving stuff. I know the boys appreciate it."

He sipped at his coffee. "How's your weekend?"

"Good. Busy." She moved a big box of floral foam to the floor. "Lots of customers yesterday, and today will be busy making the bouquets for the week."

"Do you ever take a day off?" Hendrix asked.

"I try to take a day or two a month, usually a Tuesday," she said. "It's our slowest day."

"A day or two?" The look he gave her was adorably disapproving.

"Well, it's just Carlos and me at the moment. My other employee quit and moved to Texas six months ago," Hazel said. "I've been trying to find someone else, but the pickings are slim. I did hire someone a few months ago, but she turned out to be a nightmare. It was bad. It was 'Carlos threatened to quit' level of bad."

She smiled at him. "Since then, I've been a little gun shy about hiring someone I don't know or who hasn't been recommended."

"I understand that, but working every day isn't good for you," Hendrix said.

She shrugged. "The life of a small business owner, I guess."

She reached for the last box on the shelf that held six jugs of bleach and was heavy as hell. Before she could lift it, Hendrix stood next to her. "I'll get this one."

"Thanks," she said.

She stared unabashedly at how his back muscles flexed under his shirt as he lifted the box and turned to set it on the floor. Jesus, he really did have a great body. She'd give up a kidney to see him naked just one freaking time.

"Hazel?"

"Yeah?" She dragged her gaze from what was now his chest and somehow ended up staring at his mouth. His perfect, beautiful mouth.

"You're standing in front of my toolbox."

Her face flamed, and she skittered to the side. She wanted to punch herself in the face at her idiocy. Instead, she forced another smile at Hendrix. "Sorry."

"No problem."

She busied herself with sorting through the stock as he anchored the shelf to the wall. It took him less than ten minutes, and she was strangely disappointed when he closed his toolbox and said, "All finished."

"Thank you so much, Hendrix," she said. "Really. I borrowed a drill from my friend Sierra, but I'm not much of a handyman."

"It's no problem," he said. "I'll help you put the stock back on the shelf."

"Oh no, that's all right," she said. "I'll finish it after we close tonight."

He glanced at his watch. "It's twenty after nine. If I stay and help, we can get it done before you open at ten, and you won't have to stay late tonight."

Eager to spend more time with him, even when she knew she was torturing herself, she said, "That would be great if you're sure you don't mind?"

"I don't," he said. "There's something I'd hoped to talk to you about as well."

"What's that?" She hated how cautious she sounded, but him trying to convince her they could date would only upset her and piss him off when she said no again.

"It's about Preston." He picked up the box of heavy bleach and set it on the shelf before reaching for another. "I'm sure you've noticed that he's eager to spend time with you."

She picked up some floral foam and arranged it neatly on the second shelf. "I have noticed."

He glanced at her, and she said, "It doesn't bother me if that's what you're worried about. I really like him."

He set the third box of bleach next to the others. When he didn't say anything, she said, "Preston has never mentioned his mother to me."

"Spencer hasn't told you anything about her?" Hendrix said.

She shook her head. "He hasn't, and I didn't want to pry. Don't feel like you have to -"

"Preston's mother left us when Preston was eight," Hendrix said. "She packed her clothes and stuff while I was at work, and Preston was at school. She texted me earlier, said she couldn't pick up Preston after school and asked me to do it. I said sure. When we got home, she was gone, and there was a note on the kitchen table for me. We haven't seen her since."

"Oh my God," Hazel said. "I'm sorry. That's a shitty thing for her to do. If she was unhappy in the marriage, she should have -"

"She left because two months before that, Preston came out to us as gay, and she couldn't handle having," Hendrix swallowed hard, "as she put it, a faggot for a son."

Hazel stared in shock at him, the surprise slowly turning to fury. "That bitch."

Hendrix twitched a little before nodding. "Yeah. I didn't tell Preston what the note said, and I burned the fucking thing that night so he would never get the chance to read it, but it didn't matter. He didn't have to read it. He already knew. My kid is a certified genius, but he isn't always great at reading other people's emotions or feelings. He's too preoccupied, but it isn't malicious, you know?"

She nodded. "I know."

"But he didn't need to be good at reading emotions when it came to his mom. She didn't even try to hide her... her horror and anger when Preston finally said the words 'I'm gay' to us."

"Did you know before he told you?"

"I had an idea that he might be. His mother did, too, even if she tried to deny it. Did you know Spencer was gay?"

She shook her head. "No. He told us when he was twelve. So, Preston hasn't seen or spoken to his mother since he was eight?"

"He spoke to her once," Hendrix said. "She left in October, and although she wouldn't come back to the house or tell me where she was living, she texted me every couple of weeks or so. I begged her to call Preston on Christmas Day. He missed her and...."

He paused, his throat working and his eyes becoming rimmed with red. She stepped closer and took his hands, squeezing them lightly as he cleared his throat.

"He felt so guilty about her leaving. I told him repeatedly that it wasn't his fault, but Preston is...."

"He's sensitive," Hazel said.

"He is," Hendrix said. "People don't think he is because he comes off as distant and cold sometimes, but that's just because he...."

"He gets wrapped up in his work," Hazel said. "Preston is a wonderful kid, Hendrix. He truly is. He's the perfect partner for Spencer."

He stared at their linked hands. "They do seem well matched, don't they?"

She smiled. "Yes."

"Anyway, Whitney called Preston on Christmas Day. It wasn't great. It was a mistake to ask her to call him. Preston kept apologizing to her over and over. He started crying and begging her to come back."

He paused again, and Hazel had to fight her urge to put her arms around him and hug him hard. "When he promised he wouldn't be gay anymore if she came home, I took the phone from him and ended the call."

"Oh, honey, I'm so sorry." She squeezed his hands again.

"Her leaving messed up Preston," Hendrix said. "I got him into therapy, hell, I got both of us into therapy, and I told him every damn day that being gay wasn't something he could change. It was a part of who he was, and he was perfect just as he was. I wanted him to be proud of who he was and who he loved."

"It worked," she said. "Preston isn't ashamed to be gay or feels the need to hide it."

"No, he doesn't," Hendrix said, "and I'm so fucking glad."

He rubbed his thumbs over her knuckles almost absently. "Neither of us ever spoke to Whitney again. I received divorce papers in the mail and only talked to her lawyers. It was what they called an amicable divorce."

He made a low snort of anger. "I was perfectly happy never to hear Whitney's voice again, but when Preston was sixteen, he got it in his head that he wanted to talk to her. He called the last number we had for her, but it was discon-nected. Whitney's parents had died before Preston was born, but she had a younger sister. Preston did some googling and found an address and number for her. He called Whitney's sister, but as soon as she realized who he was, she ended the call and didn't answer again."

"I'm so sorry," Hazel said.

"It's my fault," Hendrix said. "I was so blinded by my love for Whitney that I had no idea who she really was. We were married for twelve years, and I never had even an inkling that she was homophobic."

Hazel shook her head. "Look at me, Hendrix."

When he stared at her, she said, "It is not your fault. She's the monster, not you. And sometimes monsters are exceptionally good at hiding who they are. She abandoned you, and she abandoned her child over something he has no control over. That makes her the bad guy. Okay?"

He nodded. "Preston's confident and secure in who he is and who he loves, but he – well, he wants a mom. He wants to be nurtured and loved by a mother. I know he's been coming on a little strong with you."

"I don't mind," Hazel said. "I promise. I like spending time with him, and I don't care if he texts me a dozen times a day."

Hendrix groaned. "He texts you a dozen times a day?"

She smiled. "Sometimes more."

"I could talk to him," Hendrix said. "I could -"

"Don't you dare," she said. "I mean it when I say I don't mind. In fact, I love it. He's smart and funny, and I enjoy getting his texts. If Preston is looking for a mom, I'm happy to be that for him."

He studied her for a few minutes before saying, "You really mean that."

"Of course I do," she said. "I love being a mom. I wanted four kids."

He blinked. "Seriously?"

"Yep. My ex said absolutely not, so we compromised at

two, but I never got pregnant again. I wanted to try IVF, but Garrett didn't want to spend the money. Or at least, I told myself that was the reason."

"Was he upset about Spencer being gay?"

"He would have to care about Spencer to be upset." She sighed. "Shit, that was a bitchy thing to say. Spencer's dad loves him, but he was never into being a dad. You know? He wanted kids, but once Spencer came along, being a dad was either not what he thought it would be, or he'd been lying to himself about wanting kids."

"Which do you think it was?" he said.

She was still holding his hands, and she made herself let go and put a bit of space between them. "Honestly? He was lying to himself. Garrett was a very selfish person. I knew he was self-absorbed, but when I met him, my self-esteem wasn't the greatest, and I figured he was the best I deserved."

She rolled her eyes. "I have friends who wish they were twenty again, but I shudder to think about being that age. I like who I am now."

"I like who you are, too," he said.

She smiled at him and folded her arms across her torso. "I like you too, Hendrix. But it's not a good idea for us to date."

"Can you give me a better reason than, 'Spencer wouldn't like it,'? Because look, I like your kid a lot, but I don't like the idea that he has a say in who his mother dates," Hendrix said.

"I know," she said, "but my relationship with Spencer is just starting to mend, and I don't want to risk ripping it apart again. I know that sounds super dramatic, but there was a point in Spencer's life where he barely spoke to me, and I don't want to go back to that."

"I'm not getting why he would care who you date," Hendrix said.

"Normally, he wouldn't," she said. "But if I started dating you, he would see it as me trying to get closer to him, to start prying into his life again."

"He does know that you're a fully functional adult with her own feelings and needs that go beyond him, right?"

She laughed. "Yes, but to be fair, I made it difficult for him to realize that for most of his life."

"What do you mean?"

She picked at some clear tape stuck to the edge of the shelf. She didn't want to tell Hendrix what a bad mother, what a bad *person* she used to be, but she owed him a better explanation.

"I spent most of Spencer's childhood and teenage years overcompensating for Garrett's lack of interest. I mean, I took it way too far. I was way more involved in his life than I should have been, and Spencer was resentful and angry after years of it. Garrett and I separated when Spencer was thirteen. He'd barely shown any interest in Spencer when we all lived together, and it didn't get better once we divorced."

She tore off the piece of tape and rolled it between her fingers. "After Garrett moved out, I got... well, I got even worse about being in Spencer's personal space. I felt so damn guilty about his father's obvious lack of interest in him. I wanted to fix it and thought the only way to do it was by ensuring Spencer knew my world revolved around him."

She flicked the piece of tape onto the floor. "It backfired, of course. Terribly. By the time Spencer was seventeen, he wanted nothing to do with me. In fact, he moved out of the house and lived with my mom and dad while he finished his last year of high school."

"I'm sorry," Hendrix said.

She shrugged. "It was my fault. Spencer moving out was the wake-up call I needed, though. I got my ass into therapy and did some pretty intense work on myself. I did a lot of self-reflection, and while I'm still a work-in-progress, I am in a much better place now than I used to be."

She smiled at Hendrix. "Spencer didn't have much to do with me until his second year of nursing school. I called him once a month after he moved out. Sometimes he answered. Sometimes he didn't. But I'm thankful he didn't cut me out completely from his life. After a couple of years, my mom convinced him to do therapy sessions with me. Spencer got the chance to see the improvements I'd made, and he also was given an opportunity to express his anger with me. It was tough, but afterward, we both agreed to give the relationship another try."

She studied the floor for a moment, collecting her thoughts. "My relationship with Spencer is much better than it was, but I'm sure you've noticed he bristles at even the idea that I might intrude on his personal life."

"You're his mom," Hendrix said. "It's not intruding. It's caring about your kid."

"He doesn't see it that way, and that's not his fault. It's mine," Hazel said.

"Hazel, I think maybe you're a little too hard on yourself. No one is perfect and -"

She shook her head. "I need to take responsibility for my actions, and there's no shame in admitting my mistakes. Spencer sees the changes I've made, and he's expressed to me more than once how much he appreciates my efforts, but he can also be... inconsistent with his reactions to my actions. So, it means that I have to be careful about how my interest in Spencer's life looks to him. Our relationship is improving weekly, and it's even better since he and Preston started dating. Preston has pushed Spencer in a way I can't to spend time with me, and it's good for both of us, I think."

She smiled at him. "Even if I didn't already love Preston for being a good, kind man who loves my son, I would love him for how he's helped Spencer open up to me."

When Hendrix reached for her hand again, she took it, linking their fingers together. "I was upset Thursday night when it was obvious Spencer didn't want me to stay for the card game, and I was sad that he didn't ask me for help with moving Preston in next weekend. I went home on Thursday feeling pretty sorry for myself, to be honest. But the thing is, six months ago, Spencer wouldn't have even bothered to tell me that he asked Preston to move in with him. It's progress, even if it isn't as fast as I'd like. Hell, just the fact that he agreed to let me meet you is a damn miracle. He's embarrassed by me, and I know he's working on not feeling that way, but it's hard for him. He can see the changes I've made, but he also remembers me as that helicopter mom who pounced on him every time he turned around. I know I'll never be that person again, but I have to be patient and trust that eventually, he'll realize it too."

"I'm sorry that he doesn't see you for who you are now," Hendrix said.

She smiled again. "He will eventually. But right now… if we dated, I know without a doubt that Spencer would think I was only doing it to be more involved in his life. It would ruin our progress, and he'd push me away, Hendrix. I know he would. I don't want that. I don't want to go another few years where I only hear from my kid once a month."

She squeezed his hand. "I swear it has nothing to do with you. You're amazing, and I wish we could spend time together."

"Me too," he said, "but I understand why you can't."

Relief swept through her, surprising her with its intensity. She hated that Hendrix knew how badly she'd failed as a mom, but a weight she didn't know she carried had dropped away. She loathed the idea that Hendrix might think it had anything to do with him.

"You know Preston wants us to spend time together, right? He thinks if Spencer sees you with someone your age and in a 'non-mom' light, he might be more open to spending time with you," Hendrix said.

"Well, Spencer is stubborn, so I don't think Preston will get far with the four of us hanging out idea. Sadly," she gave him a teasing grin, "I am just not as cool as you, and poor Spencer is terrified you'll discover his mom is a loser."

He scowled at her. "Don't say that."

She squeezed his hand a final time before dropping it. "Thank you for being understanding about this, Hendrix. I'm sorry it's not going to work out for us. I was looking forward to getting to know you better."

"You're a good mom, Hazel," Hendrix said.

"Thank you. That means a lot." She smiled at him before glancing at her watch. "The shop opens in fifteen minutes. I'd better get a move on with this shelf."

CHAPTER 7

"Hi, are you Hazel?"

Hazel closed the cooler door and turned, smiling at the young Black woman standing behind her. She had a shaved head and a pierced lip, and she was gorgeous in an ethereal kind of way. "I am. How can I help you?"

"I'm Ruby. I'm here about the job."

"Job?" Hazel automatically took the resume Ruby handed her.

"Yes?" Ruby suddenly looked as doubtful as she did. "Um, Mr. Smith sent me?"

"Mr. Smith... Hendrix Smith?"

Ruby nodded. "Yes. My brother Jacob works with him. Mr. Smith knew I was looking for work and suggested I bring you my resume. I've worked in retail before and did all the flowers for my older sister's wedding. I don't have, like, formal education on making bouquets, but I'm pretty artistic and -"

"Ruuuuuby Red!"

Ruby turned, grinning at Carlos before fist-bumping them. "Hey, Carlos. What's happening?"

"Not much, gorgeous. How about you?" They glanced at the paper in Hazel's hand. "Are you applying for a job?"

"I am," Ruby said.

"Shit, girl, I didn't know you were looking. I would have suggested you talk to Hazel months ago. Those flowers you did for Mona's birthday bash were lit."

"You two know each other?" Hazel asked.

"Yeah," Carlos said. "We have a few classes together at the college."

"I'm working on my bachelor of art," Ruby said.

"She's got some sick skills with graphic design," Carlos said.

"Okay, well," Hazel glanced at the resume again, "do you have time to chat right now? It won't take more than half an hour."

"I do," Ruby said.

"Great, follow me." Hazel led Ruby to the back of the store.

INDIE SLAMMED HER DOOR SHUT AND HURRIED ACROSS THE parking lot. She was late for her dinner with Hazel and Sierra at Dawson's, but she'd had an end-of-the-day emergency at the clinic. She walked past the fenced-off patio. This time of year, it was too cold to sit outside, and the tables were empty, with the chairs stacked neatly against the brick wall.

She turned the corner, smiling when she saw Julia leaning against the wall a few feet from the front door. She wore her usual uniform of a plain white shirt and black pants and had her Dawson's apron tied around her waist. Her hair, a gorgeous brown so dark it looked almost black, hung down her back in a neatly made braid.

"Hey, Julia, isn't it a little cold to be taking your break outside… honey, what's wrong?"

Julia wiped at her wet cheeks. "Hi, Indie. Uh, nothing."

Indie stopped in front of her. "It's obviously not nothing. What can I do to help?"

"Nothing unless you can convince my professor to let me retake the last biochemistry exam." Julia wiped at her face again. "I had my period the day of my exam, and it was, like, so bad. My cycle has always been awful. I used to get a doctor's note for it in high school because I would have to miss a couple of days, you know?"

Indie nodded, and Julia sniffed loudly. "Anyway, I felt sick, and the cramps were excruciating, and I couldn't concentrate worth shit. I asked the professor if I could be excused and do a make-up exam, but he said he'd fail me if I left the exam."

She stared at Indie, her lower lip trembling and her pretty brown eyes wet with unshed tears. "So, I stayed, but I failed the stupid exam anyway, and it's worth forty percent of my overall grade. It's gonna lower my average, and I'll never get into medical school, and I'll be a complete failure all because I'm a w-w-woman."

She burst into tears again before throwing her arms around Indie and burying her face in her shoulder. Indie returned her hug, rubbing her back until Julia's crying slowed, and she stepped back.

"I'm sorry," Julia said.

"It's all right, honey." Indie wasn't sure of Julia's exact age, but she didn't think she was over twenty. She wiped the tears from Julia's cheeks with her thumbs. "It seems like you have a valid reason for getting a make-up exam. Could you talk to your doctor and get a note from him to give to your professor?"

"I did." Julia looked like she was about to cry again. "I emailed the professor earlier today with a copy of the note attached. He just emailed back and said if I had brought it in the day of the exam, he might have considered excusing me, but it was too late now."

"What a dick," Indie said.

"Right?" Julia took a shuddering breath. "During our last exam, one of the guys in the class left halfway through because he had a stomach ache, and Professor Rogan let him do a make-up test. He's unfair, and I don't know what to do about it."

"What about your parents?" Indie said. "Maybe they could speak with him."

"It's just my dad," Julia said. "And, like, he would talk to him, but I'm twenty. I should be able to handle my own shit, right?"

"Yes," Indie said, "but everyone needs backup sometimes. Plus, it sounds like this professor is one of those guys who… relates to men better."

Julia snorted. "If you mean he's a raging misogynistic asshole who thinks women should be barefoot and pregnant in the kitchen, then, yeah, you're right. It's ridiculous because the guy isn't, like, eighty years old. He's my dad's age."

"Well, I think you should talk to your dad about it. I know it can be embarrassing to have to talk about your period with your dad, but -"

"No, my dad is cool with that sort of stuff. It's been just him and me since I was seven, so he's been the one to do everything." Julia smiled a little. "He did all this research with me on what was, like, the best pads and tampons to use and then bought me about a dozen boxes so I would have a variety. He took me out for dinner to celebrate when I got my period for the first time."

"He sounds like a good guy," Indie said.

"He is. But I hate asking him to fight my battles," Julia said. "I'm an adult now."

Indie smoothed back a stray piece of hair from Julia's face. "Maybe think of it less as him fighting your battle and more as joining the battle. You're the general, and he's your… colonel? Captain? Lieutenant? I have no idea what rank is below general."

Julia laughed, and Indie grinned at her. "You get what I'm trying to say, though, right?"

"Yeah."

"I'm sorry you failed your exam, honey. Talk to your dad. Even if you don't want him talking to your professor, he might have some ideas on what else you can do."

"Thanks, Indie." Julia smiled at her. "You're great. You know that? You're my favourite customer."

"You're my favourite too." Indie put her arm around Julia's shoulders and squeezed her gently. "You've got this, Julia. I know you won't let some dickhead misogynist get away with screwing you over. You're too damn smart for that."

"I am, aren't I?" Julia said. She was starting to look like her usual self, and some colour had returned to her cheeks. "He's the asshole, right?"

"Totally the asshole," Indie said.

Julia leaned in and kissed her cheek. "Thanks again, Indie. You're, like, so awesome."

"So, are you, honey."

"WAIT, SO YOU JUST HIRED HER ON THE SPOT?" SIERRA stared at Hazel in disbelief, and Hazel couldn't help but grin. It took a lot to surprise Sierra.

"Hired who?" Indie slid into the booth next to Hazel. "Sorry, I'm late. There was a clinic emergency."

"No problem." Hazel smiled at her. "We told Julia you'd want your usual drink, but she hasn't brought it yet."

"Something's wrong with her tonight," Sierra said worriedly. "She's not her usual bubbly self."

"I saw her outside," Indie said. "She failed an exam because she was sick, and her professor is being a dick about letting her do a make-up one."

"Poor girl," Hazel said.

"She'll be okay, I think. I convinced her to talk to her dad about it, and if he can't help, I'll offer to talk to the professor. Sounds like he's a misogynistic asshole."

She blinked at the looks that Hazel and Sierra gave her. "What?"

"It's just a little weird to see you being so passionate about helping a Gen Z," Hazel said.

"It's Julia," Indie said. "Not some random self-absorbed kid who thinks the world revolves around them."

"Well, if you need backup, let me know," Sierra said. "I eat misogynistic guys like him for breakfast every day in court. It's what gives me my superpowers."

She made a smacking sound with her lips, and Hazel laughed. "Remind me how many lawyers have wet their pants in your courtroom?"

"Only the one, and technically it was in the jail cell after I put him in contempt," Sierra said. "Anyway, back to hiring this new girl... Rudy, you said her name was?"

"Ruby," Hazel said. "Hendrix recommended her."

"How freaking weird is it that Hendrix is Preston's dad? I

know we already discussed this last week, but I'm still trying to wrap my mind around it." Indie smiled at Julia when she brought her drink. "Thanks, honey."

"You're welcome. Are you lovely ladies having your usual?"

"We are," Hazel said.

"Awesome. I'll get your order in the system." Julia left, and Indie took a sip of her drink.

"Seriously though, it's a small world, right?"

"Yes," Hazel said.

"Made even smaller by the fact that Hendrix keeps popping by the store," Sierra said.

"Once," Hazel said. "He came by once after I said we couldn't date, and that's only because he had already agreed to help me anchor the shelf. He was just being a nice guy."

"Right. Which is why he also found you a second employee so you could stop working yourself to death... he's a nice guy," Sierra said.

"He found you a second employee?" Indie stared at Hazel.

Hazel nodded. "He did. I happened to mention that I had difficulty finding someone reliable, and he sent Ruby over on Monday to meet me. Her brother works with Hendrix."

"And you hired her?" Indie said.

"I did, but not on the spot. I called her references first and then hired her," Hazel said. "She started on Tuesday, and I know it's only Friday, but so far, she's done well. I love Carlos, and they're great with customers, but they can't design bouquets worth shit. It's just not in their wheelhouse. But Ruby is amazing at it. She's got a real eye for creating bouquets, which takes some pressure off me. Plus, she and Carlos know each other from the college and get along well."

"That's great," Indie said.

"So, you gonna thank Mr. Tall, Dark, and Handsome Electrician with a friendly game of hide the salami?" Sierra asked.

"Of course not," Hazel said, but she'd thought the same thing last night in her bed, and then masturbated to a detailed fantasy involving all the ways she said thank you to Hendrix with her mouth.

"Wow, is your face suddenly red," Sierra said. "What kind of naughtiness is your brain conjuring up?"

"It's not," Hazel lied. "I can't date him, Sierra, and you know that."

"Didn't say date." Sierra sipped at her whiskey sour. "You could just fuck him. Spencer doesn't have to know."

"I'm not looking for that," Hazel said. "I'm looking for a relationship. I'm tired of being alone."

"Hey, I get it. But what's wrong with sparking a little electricity with Hendrix while you look for your future husband?" Sierra wiggled her eyebrows at Indie. "You see what I did there, babe?"

"I saw," Indie said with a laugh.

"I'm not sure I can have sex without being emotionally involved," Hazel said. "That feels like a young woman's game to me."

"Oh yes, because you're so old." Sierra rolled her eyes. "Seriously, I'd kill to be forty-five again."

"You're forty-six, drama llama," Indie said.

"It's been one fuck of a year," Sierra said.

"Maybe if you talked to Spencer," Indie said, "he would-"

"No." Hazel shook her head emphatically before sipping at her wine. "I can't take the risk. Things are going so well with him right now. It's not perfect, but it's so much better than it was. He even called me last night and asked if I would come over tomorrow after work and help him and Preston with unpacking."

"Doesn't sound like fun," Indie said.

"It won't be. Unpacking never is. But the fact that he's willing to let me help is a great sign. I know it's partially Preston's doing, but it's also further proof that Spencer is seeing how I've changed."

Indie rubbed her arm. "He sees it, honey. I know he does."

"Anyway, I don't want to do anything to ruin the progress I've made with Spencer, which means Hendrix is strictly off-limits."

"Won't he be there tomorrow?" Sierra asked.

"No. He's helping the boys pack the U-Haul, but Preston mentioned in one of his texts yesterday that Hendrix has a prior engagement later that night," Hazel said.

She sipped at her wine again. It wasn't disappointment she felt. Hendrix not being there was for the best. Seeing him made all her good intentions about not dating him seem foggy and a bit ridiculous.

"You're bummed he won't be there," Sierra said.

Hazel wrinkled her nose. She hated how perceptive Sierra was. "I'm not."

"You're going to look a judge straight in the eye and lie. Is that what's happening here?" Sierra said.

Indie laughed, and Hazel grinned at Sierra. "Don't use your judge powers on me."

"I have no control over it. It just happens naturally. Like farting," Sierra said.

"Oh my God, my friend Marta ripped one during a chem lab last week." Julia had returned with their food. "It stunk up the whole lab, and we had to take a ten-minute break while the professor opened the windows and aired out the room. We were so proud of her."

She set their plates in front of them as Sierra laughed. "Nice work, Marta."

"Right? This guy she was crushing on asked her out the very next day. She thinks he was impressed by the fart. Enjoy your dinner."

Julia walked away, and Sierra stared at Hazel and Indie. "Is farting the new flirting?"

"Jesus, I hope not," Indie said. "I'll be single forever if it is."

"You and me both," Sierra said.

CHAPTER 8

"Mom, hey! Oh my God, I love you." Spencer grabbed the two boxes of pizza from her and the six-pack of beer before kissing her on the cheek. "Pres! My mom brought pizza and beer!"

Hazel laughed at Preston's excited whoop and followed Spencer into the kitchen. She stared in surprise at the number of boxes and kitchen accessories on the table and counter. "Wow, I didn't realize you had so many kitchen things."

Spencer balanced the pizza boxes on the narrow landing between the two sinks. "I don't. This is all Preston's. He has so much kitchen stuff. It's weird."

"It's not weird," Preston said.

"It's weird for a guy who doesn't cook," Spencer said.

"My dad buys it for me. He's determined to make me into a chef. I've told him it's never gonna happen, but he -"

"Never gives up hope."

Hendrix's deep voice directly behind her sent her pulse into overdrive. She turned, ignoring how deep her sudden delight was, and smiled at Hendrix. "Hi, Mr. Smith. I thought you were busy tonight."

"It's Hendrix, and my plans were cancelled, so I stuck around to help the boys," Hendrix said. "Is that pizza I smell?"

"Yeah, Mom brought it." Spencer dug through the cupboard for plates.

"That's very thoughtful of you," Hendrix said. "How was work today?"

"It was good, thank you." She smiled at Preston when he hugged her. "Hi, honey."

"Hey, Hazel. Thanks for helping us tonight. I know you're probably tired."

"Not at all. I'm happy to help." She *was* tired, and her feet were killing her after being on them all day at the store, but she wouldn't have missed this for anything.

Spencer handed out pizza slices, and Preston frowned when he held out a plate to Hazel. "Honey, your mom hates pineapple on pizza."

Spencer glanced at the pizza. "No, she doesn't. She always gets pineapple on pizza."

"Because you love it." Preston rolled his eyes and took the plate. "Get her a slice of the other stuff. Pepperoni and bacon with mushrooms, right, Hazel?"

"That's right," she said.

Spencer handed her a plate, and she nibbled at the pizza, trying to look charming and delicate, which proved nearly impossible with a hot slice of pizza. She was highly aware of Hendrix's large frame standing next to her. He wore a pair of jeans and a long-sleeved shirt, and there was a small smear of dirt across one perfect cheekbone.

"So, everything's moved over from Preston's apartment?" she said as Hendrix bit into his slice of pizza.

"Mostly," Spencer said around a mouthful of pizza.

"There are a few boxes left in the bedroom and the office, but we'll grab them tomorrow when we go back to clean."

"We've only just started unpacking, and I'm already regretting every shopping trip I've ever made," Preston said.

Spencer laughed. "You do have a lot of stuff for someone who spends most of his time in a lab."

"Will there even be room for all of my stuff? I have a lot of office stuff, and it'll be cramped with us sharing the office space. Shit, I really should have tried to pare down more." Preston studied the items that covered the kitchen table.

Spencer put an arm around him and kissed the side of his head. "Don't worry about it, babe. I don't mind being cramped if it means having you here with me."

Hazel glanced at Hendrix. He stared at the boys with the same goofy look of happiness she was sure was on her face. She couldn't help it, though. Seeing Spencer happy made her happy.

Too bad he doesn't care if you're happy.

She drowned that negative voice immediately. Spencer cared about her happiness. He did. She glanced at Hendrix, regret coating her like a thick layer of paint. Spencer needed time, and if she had to put her happiness on hold, so be it.

"So, I debated telling you this, but I think you need to know."

Hazel turned to see Hendrix leaning in the open doorway of Spencer and Preston's office. His arms were folded across his chest, highlighting his perfect forearms and impressive biceps, and he still had the smear of dirt across his cheekbone.

"What is it that I need to know?" She smiled and took out

another colossal-sized physics textbook from the box she was emptying.

"Until tonight, I was pretty certain you were perfect." His teasing smile took any sting out of his words.

"What did I do to shatter the illusion?" she asked.

He stepped into the room, joining her at the desk. "Pineapple on pizza. How can you hate it? It's what makes pizza so delicious."

"Ugh. You're one of those people." She placed the textbook on the empty shelf of the ceiling-to-floor bookshelf behind the desk and reached for another book in the box.

He laughed. "Those people? You mean people with discerningly good taste in pizza?"

"Sure, we'll go with that," she said.

She wiped at her forehead as she set down the textbook. "My God, the size of these books is insane."

"Tell me about it. I'm pretty sure Spencer and Preston made me lug all the book boxes into the U-Haul."

She glanced at the open doorway before lowering her voice. "Thank you so much for sending Ruby to talk to me. She's wonderful. I'm sure you know that I hired her."

"Yes," he said. "She texted Jacob right after you called her. I'm glad it's working out."

She took another glance at the doorway, keeping her voice low. "Me too. It's already made a big difference in my workload. She's a natural at making bouquets."

"You don't have to keep sneaking looks at the doorway and talking in whispers," Hendrix said. "Preston realized he'd left his laptop cord at his apartment. He and Spencer left a couple of minutes ago to pick it up."

She blushed and straightened her shirt before putting a book on the shelf. "Right. Sorry. I'm not... it's just...anyway,

Ruby is amazing, and I have you to thank for it. So, thank you."

"You're welcome," he said. "I'm happy it's helping to lessen the load. You have a lot on your plate at work."

She shrugged. "You run your own business. I'm sure you're just as busy."

He shook his head. "I don't think I am. I have admin help and an accountant. I don't work seven days a week. Running a retail store is a lot more work."

"I doubt that, but it's sweet of you to say," she said.

He studied her, and the intensity of his gaze made her feel too warm and very aware of her tits and that her underwear was dampening. Feeling stupid about her reaction to only a look, she grabbed three textbooks and heaved them out of the box. They were heavy, and she made a decidedly unsexy grunt when they caught on the box's flaps.

"Here, let me help." Hendrix stood beside her.

She sucked in a breath when his hands brushed hers. She let go of the books, wishing she could take a step back, but the wall and the desk blocked her. God, he smelled so good. He shouldn't have, he'd been lugging boxes all freaking day, but there was no denying his good clean scent made her feel a little dizzy.

Hendrix set the books on the desk and stared down at her. "Are you okay?"

"Fine." She studied the dirt on his cheek. "You have a bit of, um…."

She waved vaguely in the direction of his face.

"What?" he said.

"Uh, some dirt on your face," she said.

"Oh." He wiped at his face.

She shook her head. "No, more to the right. Your other right."

He laughed, and she hesitated before using her thumb to wipe away the dirt smudge. "There."

"Thanks," he said. "For a minute, I was worried you might do that thing where you lick me first before you clean away the dirt."

She laughed. "That's not how it works."

"Isn't it?" he said. "Although to be clear, I am perfectly happy for you to lick me if you feel the urge."

Her gaze dropped to his dick. Only for a second, but it was enough to make him grin and lean closer. "You're thinking about licking me right now. Aren't you?"

"No." Her voice was breathless and betrayed her need.

"I think about licking you, Hazel," he said. "All the time. I can't stop thinking about it. How you would taste, how you would moan, what you would sound like when you came all over my face."

"Hendrix," she whispered.

He was so close now, his warm breath washing over her face, his perfect mouth only inches from hers. It was madness, but she couldn't resist. Not when those delightful lips were right there for the licking.

Her tongue flicked across his upper lip. His low moan was muffled as he took her mouth in a soft kiss that quickly turned hard and urgent. She opened her mouth, gasping when he slipped his tongue inside to taste her.

His arm slid around her waist, pulling her up against him. She clutched at his arms, returning his kisses with an urgency that wasn't her usual style. She shouldn't be kissing him, but the boys wouldn't be back for at least half an hour, and what harm came from kissing someone?

She slipped her tongue into his mouth, moaning when he sucked on it. He took the clip out of her hair, releasing her dark locks from its grip. He tangled his big hand into her hair and held her tight as he explored her mouth.

She could feel his erection pressing against her stomach. The feel of it was intoxicating, as was his low moan when she rubbed against it.

"Fuck, what you do to me, Hazel," he groaned. He squeezed her ass through her jeans, rocking his pelvis against her as he nipped at her lower lip.

She broke the kiss when his hand slid under her shirt, staring up at him as he traced his fingers over her ribs. "This okay?"

She swallowed hard, glancing at the open doorway before nodding. "Yes."

"Good," he said, "because I am dying to touch your amazing breasts."

Her giggle died in her throat when his hand cupped her breast through her bra. His thumb rubbed along the lace at the top of the cup, and he kneaded her breast gently before he slid his hand under her bra. She moaned at the feel of his warm palm against her nipple.

When he rubbed his rough thumb pad across her nipple, she arched into him, pressing herself frantically against his hard cock before reaching down and cupping him through his jeans.

"Fuck!" He hissed out a breath before lightly pinching her nipple. "You're killing me, Hazel."

She nipped at his bottom lip, rubbing him hard through the denim. He eased his hand out from under her bra and traced the waistband of her jeans. He unbuttoned them and slipped his hand inside, running his fingers along the top of her panties.

She grabbed his wrist. "Hendrix, maybe we should -"

"I need to touch you," he breathed against her mouth. "Please, honey. I want to feel how wet you are for me."

She relented. A little because she couldn't resist the need in his voice, but mostly because she *was* wet, soaking wet, in fact, and she wanted him to know what he did to her. She released his wrist, and the sexy little grin he gave her sent fresh desire through her.

He slipped his hand inside her panties. She gripped his arms, her fingers sinking into his hard flesh when he stopped to investigate the patch of soft curls at the top of her pussy before he nudged her thighs apart with his knee and slid his hand between her legs. He kissed her, swallowing her cry of pleasure when he lightly rubbed her swollen clit.

"So wet," he whispered against her lips. "So wet and so..." he eased one finger inside her, making her cry out again, "tight."

"Hendrix." She rocked against his hand, needing friction, needing relief. "Please, I need... I..."

"I know, honey." He kissed her hard, sliding his finger out of her heat before concentrating on her clit. He worked it with soft strokes and gentle tugs, leaning back to watch her face as she moaned and gasped. "I want you to come on my hand, Hazel."

"Oh, God..." She rocked harder against his hand, her fingers pulling restlessly at his shirt as the pleasure built inside her.

He was still studying her intently and suddenly shy about showing off her o-face to a practical stranger, she buried her face into his neck, crying out with pleasure as she came in a hard rush of heat and light and bliss.

Her body shook wildly, but Hendrix's arm was a comforting iron band around her waist more than capable of supporting her trembling legs. She sucked in a gasp of air as

Hendrix kissed the side of her neck and the top of her shoulder, his fingers lightly stroking the wet lips of her pussy. "You okay?"

"Jesus, that was really good," she panted.

"It sounded good." He kissed her neck again. She was suddenly aware of his hardness against her hip. Feeling a bit selfish, she reached down and cupped his cock again.

"Sorry, that wasn't very fair to you."

He moaned lightly, his hand tightening on her hip. "Honey, I've wanted to make you come since the minute I met you."

"Oh yeah?" She rubbed him through the denim before reaching for the button on his jeans. "Right there in the flower shop?"

"Yes. I might have left so abruptly because I was this close to kissing you... with tongue."

She laughed and nuzzled his neck. "That's funny because I was this close to kissing *you*."

"We should have just fucking kissed," he groaned as she unbuttoned his jeans. "It would have saved a -"

The sound of a door slamming made them both freeze. Hazel stared at Hendrix in pure panic for three seconds before shoving away from him. She buttoned her jeans and snatched up her clip from the desk, twisting her hair and clipping it into some semblance of a bun. Hendrix had buttoned his jeans, but the telltale bulge of his erection was more than evident. He turned to face the shelf, rearranging the books she'd already put on the shelf as she grabbed one of the three books from the desk.

"Mom? We're back." Spencer stuck his head into the office. "We picked up donuts on the way home. They're in the kitchen... what's wrong?"

She smiled at him. "Nothing."

"Your face is flushed," Spencer said.

"These books are heavy." She handed one to Hendrix, who placed it on the shelf. "Thanks for the donuts."

"Yeah, no problem." Spencer stared at the back of Hendrix's head. "You sure everything is okay?"

"Just fine," Hazel said. "Although I am ready for a break." She walked around the desk and headed toward Spencer. "What kind of donuts did you get?"

"A variety," Spencer was still studying Hendrix. "You coming, Mr. Smith?"

"Be there in a minute. Just want to finish emptying this box." Hendrix half-turned and smiled at Spencer. "Save me a donut."

He looked and sounded normal, thank fucking God. Something she apparently wasn't capable of doing.

"Sure." Spencer looked at her again. "You're positive you're okay?"

"Yes." She slipped past him and headed toward the kitchen.

CHAPTER 9

Indie shoved the last of her sandwich into her mouth and chewed rapidly as she grabbed her stethoscope from her desk. She was running late for her next appointment and walked quickly out of her office, threading her way past the cat room and the examining tables. Stacy, one of the four vet techs, stood at the counter that held their lab equipment, sniffing at a urine test tube.

Indie laughed when she made a face at the smell and patted Stacy's back as she passed by. "Having a good day, Stace?"

"The best. The perfect damn urine-filled Tuesday," the vet tech said. "Your next appointment is waiting in exam room three."

"On my way." Indie wiped her mouth of any wayward sandwich crumbs before walking down the narrow hallway that housed the exam rooms. The clinic was set up so that each exam room had two doors. One that client's accessed from the front of the clinic, and a second that was for staff only to use and opened to the back of the clinic. She stopped at the back door of room three. A file holder and whiteboard were attached to the door, and she read Monica's neat hand-writing on the whiteboard.

Client: Valerie Jensen

Patient: Jack, dwarf bunny, three years old, not eating.

She hooked her stethoscope around her neck and plucked the file from the holder, opening it up and scanning Monica's notes as she opened the door.

"Good afternoon, Ms. Jensen. I'm Dr. Shaw. It's nice to meet you." She glanced up from the file, her face going bright red. The client sitting in the chair and holding a white bunny was a man. A man in a leather jacket, jeans, and a Rolling Stones t-shirt, with faded tattoos on hands twice the size of hers.

He stood, shifting the bunny to one massive hand and holding out the other. At 5'9", she wasn't short, but she suddenly felt fairy sized. He looked to be about six-five, and he had the body of a man who either did a lot of hard labour or had a monthly gym membership.

Her face hot with embarrassment, she shook his hand. A tingle of heat went through her palm, and she stared at his face. His eyes were a gorgeous dark brown. A thick brown beard with threads of silver covered his jaw. She usually liked the clean-shaven look, but the beard was neatly trimmed and suited his face perfectly. While he wasn't conventionally attractive, there was something about his mouth and those dark chocolate eyes that made her panties - to be perfectly blunt – soaking wet.

His dark hair was thick looking with more silver running through it that she found very appealing. It took all of her willpower not to study his body with frank appre-ciation.

She was still holding his hand, and more heat infused her

cheeks when he finally shook off her grip like a troublesome fly.

She cleared her throat. "I'm so sorry, Mr. Jensen. I was expecting a woman, but I, that is... I shouldn't have assumed...."

"It's fine. I get that a lot." His voice was honey-rough, and his tone suggested he thought she might be only half an idiot instead of a whole one.

"My first name is a bit different, too," she blurted. "Indiana. Uh, Indie for short. Most people think I'm named after the state, like, maybe I was conceived there or something, but I wasn't."

Indie, stop talking. Please stop talking.

"I've never even been to Indiana. I don't think my parents have, either. I was conceived right here in this town on my parents' second wedding anniversary. My dad is a huge Indiana Jones fan, though. You know the movies, right?"

He nodded, and she said, "He begged my mom to name me Indiana, and she agreed. She didn't want it shortened to Indie, but too bad because most people call me Indie. But I spell it I-n-d-i-e instead of I-n-d-y, so it's sort of different from the movie character."

She sucked in a deep breath. He didn't say anything, and she smiled weakly. "At least my last name isn't Jones, right?"

When he stayed silent, she cleared her throat again. "So, your bunny isn't eating?"

"He stopped eating the day before yesterday."

God, his deep voice made her lady bits tingle.

"Okay, let's have a look at him."

He set the rabbit on the exam table between them. She did a quick exam before palpating the bunny's abdomen. "There's a lot of gas in his belly. You said the last time he ate was two days ago?"

"Yes. I gave Jack fresh hay in the morning and his scoop of pellets. He ate in the morning, but when I came home from work that night, he wouldn't eat the veggies I gave him. Didn't eat anything yesterday or this morning."

"Have you noticed if he's passing any stool?"

"Not as much as he usually does." He reached out, and Indie had a rather inappropriate reaction to watching him stroke the bunny's head and ears.

"Jack is a cute name," she said to distract herself from imagining what it would be like to have his hands stroking *her*.

"My daughter named him. He's her rabbit, but she couldn't have him in her dorm room at the university."

"Ah." She stroked the bunny's sleek back, not liking how he was hunched into a loaf shape or occasionally ground his teeth. "Bunnies can often go into what we call gut stasis. Basically, nothing is moving through his digestive tract. It's a serious condition that can be fatal."

She pinched the skin between Jack's shoulder blades, lifting the fold of skin and then releasing. "Normal hydrated skin should bounce back quickly. You can see that his skin stays tented. Jack's quite dehydrated, which is common when they go into stasis. Based on his appearance, Jack is a very sick rabbit."

His big hand smoothed across Jack's head. "How sick?"

"The likelihood of him dying without treatment is high. That being said, he's only three and, overall, in good shape. The chance of recovery from stasis with treatment is excellent. I recommend that he stay with us for at least twenty-four hours in the clinic. I want to do an x-ray to confirm there are no blockages in his intestines. He'll need IV fluids, pain relief meds, gastric motility medication to get his gut moving again, and force-feeding every few hours until he starts eating on his own. I can do an estimate for you on the cost."

She petted the rabbit's soft fur and waited resignedly for what she knew would happen. The cost of the rabbit's treatment would be high, and many people considered rabbits to be disposable pets. This man would be no different. Frankly, she was surprised he'd even brought the rabbit to the clinic. There was no chance he would approve treatment. She would suggest doing the bare minimum - sub-q fluids and sending him home with Critical Care and a demonstration on how to force feed Jack, but she doubted he'd even be willing to pay for that. If he didn't, the best she could do then was suggest euthanasia so the rabbit wouldn't suffer horribly over the next few days.

"All right," he said.

She forced a smile. "Mr. Jensen, I could cut costs by not doing an x-ray, giving him some fluids under the skin, and showing you how to force feed... wait, what did you say?"

He studied her with those beautiful dark eyes. "We'll do what you're recommending. Do I pay the entire cost upfront or just a deposit?"

"Oh, um, a deposit, but the receptionist at the front will take care of that." Suddenly ashamed by her assumptions of him, she said, "I'll make up the estimate, and you can look it over and sign off on it. In the meantime, we'll get treatment started for Jack."

He nodded before petting the rabbit again with an affectionate look tinged with worry. Feeling even more ashamed by her preconceived notions of the silent Mr. Jensen, she picked up Jack and carried him to the back.

"So, HE APPROVED TREATMENT FOR THE RABBIT. EVERYTHING you suggested?" Hazel sipped at her wine.

Indie nodded. "He did. And he called the clinic right before I left tonight to ask how he was doing."

"Okay, well, that's adorable." Sierra took a healthy swallow of her whisky sour. "So, how hot was this Valerie Jensen?"

"That's the thing," Indie said. "He wasn't exactly handsome, but there was something about him."

Her usually pale cheeks were flushed, and Hazel couldn't remember the last time she'd seen Indie this animated about a guy.

"I mean, he was huge and scary looking, and growing up with a name like Valerie, you know he's gotta be tough as nails," Indie said.

"That's definitely a man who's been in more than a few fights," Sierra said.

"Right? But he was so gentle with the bunny and... I don't know. I was just... I made a fool of myself in front of him. That's about all I know for certain," Indie said with a soft sigh.

Hazel shook her head. "You're too hard on yourself, honey. I'm sure you were perfectly professional."

"Except for the part where you talked about your parents banging you into existence," Sierra said.

Indie groaned, and Hazel laughed. "Yeah, except for that part. How's the bunny doing?"

"Good," Indie said. "No blockages, and he's responding well to treatment. We're still force-feeding him, but hopefully, by tomorrow, he'll be eating on his own."

"That's great," Hazel said.

"As much as I love all the bunny and his big, bad owner, who Indie most obviously wants to fuck conversation, let's talk about what Hazel is hiding from us," Sierra said.

"I'm not hiding anything," Hazel said.

"I don't want to fuck him," Indie said.

"Fuck who?" Julia asked as she stopped at their table with fresh drinks and their meals.

Indie shook her head. "Never mind, you. How's the situation with your professor?"

Julia's face lit up. "He has to give me a make-up exam. I talked to my dad about it on the weekend, and he suggested I file a formal complaint with the department. He helped me write the complaint, and I submitted it yesterday morning. Turns out, this dickhead professor has done this in the past to other women. It's, like, the fourth or fifth complaint he's had about this exact thing. So, he got in trouble, and now he has to give me a second chance on the exam."

"That's awesome. I'm really happy to hear that," Indie said.

"Thanks, me too. Enjoy your dinner, ladies." Julia walked away, and Hazel shoved a French fry into her mouth as Sierra stared at her.

"Spill it, Hazel."

"Nothing to spill," Hazel said.

"Indie," Sierra said, "you might want to sit with me on this side of the booth before Hazel's flaming pants catch you on fire too."

Indie snorted laughter, and Hazel chucked a French fry at Sierra. She caught it in her mouth and grinned at Indie and Hazel's identical gasps of surprise. "What? I'm good at mouth stuff."

She chewed and swallowed before pointing at Hazel. "You might as well tell us. You know I'll get it out of you before you finish dinner anyway."

Hazel sighed. "I made out with Hendrix on Saturday night at Spencer's apartment."

"Shut the fuck up," Sierra said.

"I thought he wasn't going to be there," Indie said.

"He wasn't, but then his thing got cancelled, and then Spencer and Preston left the apartment for a bit, and the next thing I knew, I was kissing Hendrix, and his hand was down my pants." Hazel drank a big swallow of wine and stared at her plate of food.

Sierra leaned forward. "Oh, don't stop now, girl. This shit just got interesting."

"WOW, SO," INDIE LOOKED AROUND THE CROWDED restaurant before lowering her voice, "he made you come that easily, huh? I wish I could be that relaxed with a new boyfriend."

"Sweetheart, I keep telling you that your scum of an ex-husband was the problem in bed, not you," Sierra said in an exasperated tone.

"Oh yeah? Because I've slept with five other men since him, and none of them could make me come," Indie said. "I think that proves you're wrong."

"No, it proves that he's still in your fucking head, insisting that any of your sex problems fall squarely on your shoulders when it clearly was him and his inability to please a woman."

Indie shook her head before glancing at Hazel. "Sorry, this is about you and your fabulous new guy, not me and my sex issues."

"He's not my fabulous new guy," Hazel said. "Nothing

has changed. We can't date, and just because we got a little carried away doesn't mean it will happen again."

"Doesn't mean it won't either," Sierra said. "Obviously, the two of you have smoking chemistry, and you can't tell me there isn't a part of you that wants to return the orgasm favour. The poor guy has a raging case of blue balls now. You just going to let that happen?"

Hazel muttered a curse before pushing away her empty plate. "I do feel bad about that. He gave me an incredible orgasm, and I didn't do anything for him."

"Bad timing about the boys coming home," Indie said. "Maybe you could stop at his place and offer to blow him."

"I can't. Knowing my luck, Spencer and Preston would drop by or something," Hazel said. "Look, I want to get my mouth around that magnificent dick as much as the next girl, but it's not going to happen. Saturday night was an accident. I won't let it happen again."

"Oh yeah? Because I feel like the second you see him, you're going to be offering him happy dick time with your mouth," Sierra said.

"Sierra!" Hazel said.

"Am I wrong?"

"Probably not," Hazel said.

Sierra and Indie laughed. Hazel sighed loudly. "I have to stay away from him. It's the only thing I can do."

"That's not going to work," Indie said. "Especially if Preston is determined to get the four of you to hang out regularly."

"I don't think Spencer is ready for that to happen yet," Hazel said. "So, maybe if a few weeks go by, I'll forget how amazing Hendrix is at making me come, and by the time I see him again, I'll be able to act normal around him. Right?"

When neither Indie nor Sierra replied, Hazel scowled at them. "Say I'm right, you guys."

"You're right," Indie said doubtfully.

"You're totally right," Sierra said. "It's the perfect plan."

She looked at Indie and stage whispered, "Did that sound like I meant it?"

"I kind of hate you right now, Sierra," Hazel said.

Sierra laughed. "Babe, you fucking love me."

CHAPTER 10

"Hey, Indie? Jack's owner is here. God, that guy is a brute, huh? He could break me in half without working up a sweat." Monica leaned against the exam table.

Indie checked the beagle's mouth a final time before stroking her head. Mollie's tail thumped happily against the steel table. "Mollie's teeth look great. Tell Lorraine that Mollie has healed nicely from the dental and to keep up the good work with the brushing."

"Sure." Monica picked up the beagle, grinning when Mollie licked her cheek. "Mr. Jensen is in exam room two waiting for the demonstration on force-feeding Jack. Do we have any leftover Critical Care I can use, or do I need to make a new batch?"

"Actually," Indie willed herself not to blush, "I'll show Mr. Jensen how to force-feed Jack."

"You sure?"

"Yes. Can you prep Ranger for his neuter once you're finished with Mollie?"

Monica nodded before heading toward the front of the clinic. Indie quickly made up a fresh batch of Critical Care, grabbed a large syringe, and opened Jack's kennel. She carried the bunny to the exam room, knocking briefly before opening the door.

"Hello, Mr. Jensen."

"Hey, doc."

Today he wore jeans and a Prism t-shirt. There was a bit of black grease on the front of his shirt and embedded in the small lines on his hands. He must have seen her staring at his hands because he self-consciously wiped them on his jeans. "Just came from the shop."

"Are you a mechanic, Mr. Jensen?" She set Jack down on the exam table, placing the bowl of Critical Care and syringe next to him. She told herself she was being polite and making small talk, not grilling a man she'd never see again for personal information.

"Val," he said.

"I'm sorry?" She kept one hand on Jack's back to stop him from hopping off the table.

"Call me Val." He joined her at the table, petting Jack's head with one big hand.

"Oh, okay," she said. Her usual low voice was a little high-pitched. Jesus, he smelled good. Did all mechanics smell this good? Shouldn't they smell like oil and grease and car parts?

She was staring at him like a love-struck teenager, for God's sake. She cleared her throat. "So, Jack is doing much better. He ate some hay on his own this morning and has started passing stool regularly. His abdomen feels softer, and he isn't in as much pain."

"That's good." Val petted Jack's ears, a small smile crossing his face when Jack flattened his chin to the table.

"He does that because he's asking to be groomed," Indie said.

"Yeah, I know." He rubbed Jack's head before studying the bowl of Critical Care. "I need to feed him that?"

"Ideally," she said. "My recommendation is to force-feed him a few more times this evening even though he's eating on his own. It's important that we keep Jack's gut moving. Critical Care will help a great deal. If you're okay with force-feeding him?"

Val shrugged. "Sure."

Surprised again but determined not to show it this time, Indie said, "Great. I'll be sending him home with some pain relief meds as well. I'll demonstrate how to force-feed him and if you have any questions, just ask."

She showed Val how to feed Jack the Critical Care. He paid close attention, and she was pleased to see how well he did when he tried it on his own. Of course, it helped that Jack obviously loved him and was much more patient about Val force-feeding him.

"Okay, well, I think that's it," she said once she'd gone over the pain med schedule with him. "It's important for the next forty-eight hours to closely monitor Jack and ensure he's eating and passing stool. If he does stop eating again at any point, force feed him some Critical Care and then call the clinic."

"Thanks, doc." Val held out his hand, and she shook it, another quiver of awareness running through her pussy when their hands connected. When his gaze dropped to her mouth, she swallowed hard, her hand squeezing around his.

"You're welcome." Her voice came out soft and breathy like maybe she wanted him to kiss her.

He held her hand, his gaze arrowed in on her mouth. He had beautiful long eyelashes. She could only achieve that length with false ones and a few coats of mascara. She leaned closer, the table's edge digging into her stomach, and parted her lips a little. Maybe if she made it clear that she wanted him to kiss her, he would –

There was a knock on the door before it opened. Indie jumped like she'd been shot in the back. Val dropped her hand, and she turned, smiling guiltily at Monica. "Hi, what's up?"

"Sorry to interrupt," Monica said, "but Dr. Armstead needs your assistance. I can finish up with Mr. Jensen."

"No need. We're just finishing now. I'll be right there." She waited until Monica had closed the door before turning to face Val again. "So, I'll send you home with a bag of Critical Care and the meds. If you have any problems…."

"Call the clinic, got it." Val was petting Jack again and definitely not looking at her mouth. Hell, he couldn't seem to look at her at all.

"Yes. And, um…"

What are you doing, Indie? Don't do it, girl. Jesus, please don't do it.

"I'll put my cell number on the discharge notes. If Jack stops eating after clinic hours or if you, uh, need anything else from me… just call. I always have it with me."

He finally looked at her, the surprise on his face making her feel stupid. Did she really think he would be interested in her? They were about as different as two people could be.

Finally! She sees the light! A little too fucking late, of course.

"Okay," he said slowly. "Thanks again."

"You're welcome. Nice to meet you, Mr. – Val. It was nice to meet you, Val."

He nodded, and her face hot and stomach churning, she left the exam room.

"SIERRA, ARE YOU OKAY?" HAZEL STUDIED HER BEST FRIEND in the dim light of the restaurant.

"Fine. Tired and have a bit of a headache. I was sanding the guest bedroom walls last night and think my dust mask was faulty. My sinuses are killing me." Sierra leaned back in the booth and rubbed her forehead before smiling at Indie. "No word from hot bunny dude yet?"

Indie groaned and drank a large swallow of wine. "No. God, what was I thinking? I can't believe I gave him my number. He's not gonna call me."

"He might call," Hazel said.

"It's been a week," Indie said. "He's not going to call."

"Who isn't going to call?" Julia set fresh drinks in front of them.

"Hot guy that Indie wants to bang," Sierra said.

"Sierra!" Indie glared at Sierra.

Julia laughed and held out her fist. "Nice. Get it, girl."

Indie bumped her fist. "Thanks, but I am not getting it. He never called, and it's been a week."

"He's an asshole then," Julia said. "You're crazy hot. You're also one of the smartest people I know, and your tits are, like, incredible."

Hazel and Sierra laughed as Indie's mouth dropped open. "Uh, thanks, I think?"

"Oh, it's a compliment," Julia said. "The guy's stupid not to call you, which means you're better off without him. You need to find a man who will worship you – all of you."

"God, I wish I'd figured that out when I was twenty," Sierra said.

Julia shrugged. "My dad drilled it into me that while it's nice when a guy tells you you're pretty, it's more important that he admires your brains and the qualities that make you a good person."

"Smart guy," Sierra said.

"He is." Julia smiled at Indie. "Don't worry about that idiot, Indie. Your Mr. Right will come along. I know it."

She walked away, and Hazel smiled at Indie. "She's such a sweet kid."

"She really is," Indie said. "I don't have the heart to tell her that I'm not looking for Mr. Right, but rather Mr. Let's Just Fuck and Not Talk."

Sierra held up her glass. "Nothing wrong with a booty call lifestyle, babe."

Indie clinked her glass against Sierra's, and they both drank.

Hazel's phone vibrated, and she dug it out of her purse, reading the text on her screen. "Holy shit."

"What's wrong?" Sierra asked.

"It's Spencer. He…"

"Is he okay?" Indie's hand tightened on her wine glass, alarm crossing her face.

"Yeah, he's fine." Hazel stared at Sierra and Indie. "He invited me to go with him and Preston to Hendrix's cabin next weekend."

"That's awesome," Indie said.

"Hendrix is going too."

"Ruh-roh," Sierra said.

Hazel drank the last of her wine and reached for the fresh glass. "I can't go."

"You have to go," Sierra said.

"I can't. Not with Hendrix there. Not when he gave me an orgasm in … oh my God." Hazel drank two large swallows of wine. "I'll tell Spencer I would love to go, but I can't get away from work. I mean, there's no way I can leave the shop for a weekend. I have bouquets to make on Sunday and -"

"Didn't you say that Ruby was excellent at making bouquets?" Sierra said.

"Yes, but…"

"Honey, Sierra's right. You have to go," Indie said. "This could be a game changer in your and Spencer's relationship. He's asking you to spend an entire weekend with him."

"But Hendrix -"

"Screw Hendrix," Sierra said. "Well, not really because you refuse, but this weekend is about your relationship with Spencer. You've been waiting for something like this for years. You cannot say no."

"Besides, it won't be like you and Hendrix will be alone. Preston and Spencer will be there," Indie said.

Hazel took a deep breath, trying to quell the weird panic in her stomach. "You're right, of course, you're right. I have to do this. Okay, I'm texting Spencer right now."

"You've got this, babe," Sierra said. "It's gonna be a great weekend."

CHAPTER 11

"Hazel, make sure you pack warm clothes. The cabin's in the mountains, and it's colder there."

Spencer laughed and punched Preston lightly in the arm. "Honey, relax. My mom is a grown woman. She knows how to pack for the weather."

Hazel sank into the kitchen chair, smiling at both of them. "I'm packed appropriately for the weather. Don't worry, Preston."

"Okay, I just wanted to check. My dad said it might snow Saturday morning, so bring your winter boots," Preston said.

Spencer rolled his eyes as Hazel smiled again. "I will. Is your dad there already?"

"Yeah, he went up this morning. He had a few things to do around the cabin before we get there tomorrow night. Are you sure you're okay driving by yourself? Spencer's shift finishes at eight-thirty. If you want to wait and drive with us, that's perfectly fine. The roads can be a little slippery."

"Pres, babe, seriously, you gotta relax." Now Spencer's voice held a note of exasperation. "My mom is fine to drive by herself. Right?"

He gave her a 'say what I want to hear' look that reminded her of his dad. She forced a smile and said, "No problem. I'll leave at six when the store closes and be waiting for you at the cabin when you arrive."

"Cool. You and my dad can, like, play crib or something," Preston said.

She kept her smile glued into place with sheer willpower. Playing crib was the last thing she wanted to do with Hendrix. The things she *wanted* to do with him would horrify her son and Preston.

She wished she had known about Spencer working so late on Friday before telling them she would drive to the cabin Friday evening. She would have waited until Saturday morning to leave if she'd known. It was a two-hour drive to the cabin, which meant if Preston and Spencer didn't get there until ten-thirty, she would have almost three hours of alone time with Hendrix.

Her pulse sped up, and a little rush of pleasure flooded her stomach. She ignored it. She might be able to think of some enjoyable things she could do to Hendrix during their alone time, but, ultimately, it was a terrible idea. Having sex with Hendrix, hell, just giving him a blow job, would make her want more. She couldn't have more.

It'd been almost two weeks, and despite her best efforts, she couldn't stop thinking about him. But she hadn't seen or heard from Hendrix since that night at the boys' apartment. She'd hoped he would stop at the shop to say hello, but he hadn't. Maybe he was pissed that she hadn't tried to contact him to at least return the orgasm favour. She wouldn't blame him if he were.

Her mind whirling, she didn't realize Preston was calling her name until Spencer poked her in the arm.

"Sorry, what?"

Preston smiled at her. "I was saying how happy we are that you could get time off at the store to come to the cabin. This weekend will be great. Right, Spence?"

"It will," Spencer said. "We should probably get going. You have to be at the university early."

"Sure. Just going to use the washroom before we go." Preston left the kitchen.

Hazel waited until she heard the guest bathroom door shut before she said, "Thank you for inviting me, honey. I'm looking forward to it."

"It was Preston's idea," Spencer said.

Her glued-on smile slipped despite her best efforts. Guilt crossed Spencer's face, making her feel worse. He cleared his throat. "I mean, I want you to come too. I'm glad you are."

"It'll be nice to get away for a couple of days," she said.

"Yeah. Hey, so, um, I know you've been awesome at giving me space, and I appreciate it, I do, but," he glanced at the kitchen doorway, "you'll play it cool at the cabin, right? You won't get weird or clingy or ask too many personal questions to Preston or me or his dad?"

"I'll be so cool, the snow will be jealous," she said, keeping her tone light.

He laughed before giving her another fleeting guilty look. "Maybe try not to talk that much. All right?"

"Sure," she said as bile burned the back of her throat. "I'll be on my best behaviour."

He hesitated, scratching compulsively at his forearm as his foot tapped out a nervous beat on the floor. She reached out and placed her hand over his, stopping the jerky movements. "Say what you need to say, Spencer."

He sucked in a deep breath. "I'm happy you're coming to

the cabin, but I don't want you to see this trip as an invitation to insert yourself back into my life. I'm worried you'll start smothering me again."

His words carved a jagged hole through the center of her heart. She reminded herself that it was better for him to be honest with her than to shut her out of his life completely.

"I understand, and I promise I won't use this trip to force a change in our relationship. I know your boundaries, and I won't cross them," she said.

"I'm not trying to be an asshole," he said.

"I know. I appreciate your honesty." She squeezed his arm before releasing it and curling her hands around the mug. "Preston said you guys sometimes snowshoe when you're at the cabin?"

"We do." Preston had returned. "My dad taught me when I was a kid, and I taught Spencer last winter. I can get my dad to teach you this weekend if you want?"

"Maybe," Hazel said as Spencer stood.

"Okay, well," Preston leaned down and kissed her cheek, "we'll see you … hey, you okay? You look upset."

"Not at all." Hazel smiled at him. "Just thinking about whether I should pack an extra pair of long underwear if I'm learning to snowshoe."

Preston laughed. "Probably a smart idea. We'll see you tomorrow night at the cabin."

"You bet. Bye, guys."

"Bye, Mom," Spencer said.

"Bye, Hazel." Preston's grin was as gleeful as a little kid's. "This weekend is gonna be awesome."

She waited until she heard Spencer's car driving away before letting the hot tears fall.

HAZEL PEERED THROUGH THE BLINDING, DRIVING SNOW AS she inched along the slippery mountain road, her fingers ice cold and aching from clenching the steering wheel. The blizzard was some weird combination of ice pellets and snow, and the beleaguered windshield wipers made a squealing, moaning sound that felt like a nail hammered directly into her brain.

They squealed again, and she made a small moaning gasp when the car slid down the small hill she'd just barely managed to crest.

Fuck. She hated winter driving as it was, and these were the worst road conditions she'd ever seen. The blizzard had hit quickly and savagely. Already halfway up the mountain, unsure if it was better to continue or turn back, she'd decided to keep going. A decision she sincerely regretted.

Keeping her eyes glued to a road she could barely see, she rolled her shoulders, trying to ease some of the tension. Spencer and Preston would be trying to drive in this, too, if she didn't warn them.

She glanced at the clock on the dashboard. It was almost eight. At Carlos' urging, she had left at five instead of six, but the storm had eaten up any extra time she might have gained. Eaten it up and spit it out, and added an extra hour of driving for good measure.

She glanced at her useless phone sitting on the passenger seat. She'd lost reception surprisingly fast, even before the storm got bad. When – *if* – she made it out of this alive, she was switching to a different provider.

She sucked in a breath and released it harshly. She squinted out the windshield, staring steadily at a spot to her right. She thought she'd seen a light. She made a shaky little laugh of relief when she rounded a corner and saw the light again. It was emanating from a cabin set back in the trees. The cabin was a small log building straight out of the pages of *Little House on the Prairie* and the first sign of life she'd seen since she turned onto the road that led up to Hendrix's place. If Preston's directions were correct, it was their cabin.

She slowed the car to a crawl, looking for a driveway and almost crying with relief when she saw a section of snow that looked like it might have been shovelled in the last couple of hours. She turned into the driveway, her tires spinning, and parked in front of the cabin. She didn't see Hendrix's work truck but a small and compact SUV.

She was probably at the wrong cabin, but she didn't care. She'd rather face the potential serial killer who may live in that cabin than keep driving. Before they chopped her up into tiny bits, she'd ask if she could borrow their phone to call Spencer and tell him to keep his ass off this horrible mountain.

She shut off the car, shoved her phone into her jeans pocket, and opened her door. Freezing wind buffeted her from all sides, whipping her hair around and driving little ice pellets painfully into her skin. The cabin door opened, and she sagged with relief against the side of her car when she saw Hendrix.

Pulling on a jacket, he hurried down the porch steps and waded through the shin-deep snow to her. "Hazel!" His ears were already turning red with the cold. "Honey, what are you doing here?"

"I…" her teeth were chattering, and she couldn't get her voice to work properly. "I… invited."

"Come inside before you freeze to death." Hendrix opened the back door and grabbed her suitcase before slamming the door shut. He took her hand, and she followed him up the steps and into the warm cabin.

He shut the door and locked it while she took off her boots. He hung her jacket on the hook as she stared at the cabin. It was one giant room with the kitchen and living room separated by a large island topped with butcher block. There were three doors leading off the living room and stairs leading to a loft. The door on the far left was partially open, and she could see a small glass shower and part of the vanity. It was more modern inside the cabin than she imagined, and she studied the gleaming kitchen as Hendrix hung his jacket next to hers. Something delicious smelling was cooking on the stove in a large steel pot.

"C'mon, honey." Hendrix led her into the living room. A fire crackled in the stone fireplace, and, at Hendrix's urging, she sank onto the large grey sectional in front of it.

Her lips weirdly numb, she said, "Sp-p-pencer and P-p-preston. Need to call. Tell them not to come. Warn them."

She clutched at Hendrix. "Phone them. P-ph-phone them right now."

"They're not coming, honey. It's okay," he said. "I called and warned them about the blizzard before the power went out."

There were lights on in the kitchen and the living room, and when he saw her staring at them, he said, "I turned on the generator to make some dinner."

"I saw the light," she said. "I saw the light in the snow."

He rubbed her arm as she stared at the fire. She wasn't cold, but her entire body trembled, and her hands shook so badly she couldn't even pull her phone out of her pocket.

She lifted her hands and showed them to Hendrix. "I'm not cold. Why can't I stop shaking?"

"It's the adrenaline." He hesitated before pulling her into her arms. "You're okay now, Hazel. You're safe. Take some deep breaths."

She buried her face in his shoulder, breathing deeply as Hendrix massaged her tense upper back and shoulders. After about five minutes, she lifted her head and managed a weak smile. "Better, thank you."

"You're welcome." He kept his arm around her, and she leaned against him. She might have stopped shaking, but she wasn't ready to leave Hendrix's warm and reassuring bulk.

"Are you sure Spencer and Preston won't try to drive up here?" she asked.

"Yes. They're safe, Hazel. Why did you drive it?" Hendrix said. "Preston said they would call you, and it was only a little after six. You would have barely been out of the city."

She laughed shakily. "I left the store early. I started driving at five. By six, I was in the mountains, and the storm was already bad. I had no reception, so I didn't get any calls."

"Shit," Hendrix said. "I'm sorry."

"I didn't know if I should turn back or keep going. I kept going, hoping the storm would lessen. It didn't. It got worse and worse, and the roads were so bad."

She shuddered again, and Hendrix squeezed her tightly before pressing a kiss against her forehead. "You're here now, and you're safe."

"Safe," she repeated before taking another deep and shaky breath as Hendrix pulled his phone from his pocket and stared at it.

"No reception?" she said.

"No, I didn't expect to have any, but I wanted to double-check. With the storm, the landline isn't working either."

"What does it matter?" she asked. "Spencer and Preston aren't driving here. It's fine."

"They'll be worried about you," he said. "We have no

way of letting them know you're safe until the storm ends and the landline comes back."

"Spencer won't be worried about me," she said.

He frowned at her. "He will, Hazel."

She shook her head and sat up, tucking her hands between her thighs and staring into the fire. "He won't be. They weren't expecting me to leave until six, and, as you said, I would have barely been out of the city by then."

"Yeah, but if you didn't answer his call or text, he'd be -"

"I don't respond right away to his texts. He doesn't like it if I show too much eagerness to talk to him. He won't be worried until tomorrow, and even then, I don't think he'll be too concerned if I haven't replied. He'll think I went into the shop and got busy."

Hendrix scowled. "I don't believe your son won't be worried when he doesn't hear from you."

She shrugged and made herself smile at him. "We don't have the kind of relationship you and Preston do. Look, it's fine, all right? Don't stress about it. I guarantee you that Spencer isn't giving it a second thought."

She hesitated, realizing how that made Spencer sound and hurried to correct herself. "He's not selfish. He's a great kid, very thoughtful and caring. It's what makes him such a good nurse."

"He doesn't extend that thoughtfulness or caring to you," Hendrix said.

"It's my fault," Hazel said. "I was too -"

"Yeah, I know," Hendrix said. "You've already told me why you think it's your fault."

He stood and added another log to the fire before glancing at her. "Supper will be ready soon. Do you want to have a shower first? I'll need to shut off the generator once the food is ready."

"Yes," she said. "I won't be long."

He picked up her small suitcase and carried it toward one of the closed doors. "I'll set you up in the guest room. There are extra towels in the closet."

CHAPTER 12

"I can wash the dishes," Hazel said.

Hendrix cleared away the plates, setting them in the sink and waving off her attempt to help. "I'll clean up tomorrow when the storm is over and the power is back on."

"Thank you for dinner. It was delicious," Hazel said.

"You didn't eat very much." His tone was worried rather than accusing.

She sipped at her wine. "Leftover nerves from the drive affected my appetite, I guess."

That was only partially the truth. Her appetite had diminished because now that she knew Spencer and Preston were safe, her need for Hendrix had come roaring back to life.

She knew she didn't imagine the sexual tension between them, nor had she imagined the way Hendrix's gaze had repeatedly dipped to her braless tits.

She hadn't brought anything sexy to wear to bed, but when she'd put on her cotton pajamas after her shower, she'd skipped the bra and the panties. Not because she was trying to seduce Hendrix now that they had an entire evening alone, but because it was more comfortable.

Keep telling yourself that, Hazel.

"Are you warm enough?" Hendrix asked. He'd shut off the generator as soon as he finished cooking, and they'd eaten dinner by candlelight and firelight. His gaze dropped to her breasts again, where she could practically feel her nipples straining at the soft cotton. Her hard nipples had nothing to do with being cold and everything to do with her picturing Hendrix sucking on them.

"Yes," she said. "The cabin is warm even without the generator. The fireplace throws off more heat than I thought."

"It helps that the place is small," Hendrix said. He leaned against the counter, folding his arms across his chest. He'd pushed his sleeves up, and she stared at his bare forearms in the dim light and those rough hands that knew how to touch her so perfectly.

"It's small but really lovely," she said.

"I'd give you a tour, but it's dark, and you've already seen most of it," he said with a small smile. "The loft upstairs is Preston's room, and that door leads to my bedroom."

They sat silently for a moment before Hendrix said, "Do you want more wine?"

She studied her mostly empty glass. "Yes, why not? It's not like we're going anywhere tonight, right?"

"Not in this storm." Hendrix poured more wine into her glass before pouring himself some. "Let's sit on the couch."

She followed him to the couch, sinking into the soft leather and studying the flickering flames as Hendrix added another log and poked around in the fire with the poker, setting off small sparks, snaps, and crackles.

"There's something comforting about a wood fire, isn't there?" Hazel said. "I have a gas fireplace at the house, but I've always loved a wood fire."

"Me too," Hendrix said.

"Maybe when I downsize, I'll look for a condo with a wood fireplace," she said with a grin. "I'm sure they exist, right?"

He laughed and sat beside her, his thigh close to hers but not quite touching. "It might be difficult to find one."

The howling wind rattled the windows, but the sound didn't bother Hazel. Not when she was safe and warm in a gorgeous cabin with the perfect man.

He is perfect. You should fuck him.

She cleared her throat as Hendrix said, "So, you're thinking of downsizing?"

"I am. The house is too big for one person. I should have sold it years ago, but it was Spencer's childhood home, and I wanted him always to feel like he had a place to come home if he needed."

She smiled at him. "But a smaller mortgage would make a big difference for me. I could travel, maybe take more than a day or two off from the shop every month. Participate in that work-life balance thing I've heard so much about."

He laughed. "You deserve to travel and not work so many hours. Where would you go first?"

"Hawaii," she said. "I've never been there."

"It's a beautiful place. I took Preston to Oahu when he was fifteen. We had a great time. The only trip he liked more was when we backpacked across Europe two years later."

"You've been to Europe? I'm jealous," she said. "I've spent my whole life wanting to travel."

"Then you should," Hendrix said. His gaze lingered on her mouth. "You should do what you want, Hazel."

She took his wine glass and set it on the coffee table along with hers. "I want to kiss you."

His smile could have dimmed the sun. When she leaned forward, he met her halfway, not the least bit embarrassed by his obvious eagerness. He cupped the back of her neck and kneaded lightly as they explored each other's mouths. She loved the way Hendrix kissed. Gentle, coaxing brushes of his mouth against hers that made her feel both cherished and desperate for more.

She slid closer to him on the couch, and he put his arm around her, pulling her up snugly against him as he continued to explore her mouth with those slow and almost lazy kisses. One hand still kneaded her neck, the other stroked lightly along her thigh. He hadn't made any effort yet to go beyond kissing, and she loved every minute of it, even if her breasts felt heavy and swollen and her pussy ached and throbbed with the need to be filled.

Her ex had grown perfunctory in their lovemaking only a few years into the marriage. She'd forgotten what it was like to be this worked up by just a few kisses, forgotten how delicious the anticipation of sweeter things could be.

When Hendrix's tongue invaded her mouth again, she sucked hard on it. He groaned, squeezing her thigh before he slid his hand up to her breast and cupped it through her shirt. She arched into him, gasping when he kissed his way down her throat and nipped at her collarbone.

He teased her nipple through her shirt, and she moaned his name, clutching his shoulders. When he reached for her shirt, she helped him drag it over her head, tossing it on the floor.

"So fucking beautiful," Hendrix said in a low voice before pushing her onto her back on the couch. He leaned over her and sucked on her right nipple, forcing another cry of pleasure from her throat. She wound her hands into his hair, holding tight as he teased her nipples until they ached, and her hips rose and fell against him.

"Your breasts are amazing," Hendrix said as he blazed a path of kisses along her collarbone and between her breasts.

"Th-thank you," she gasped. She pulled at his shirt, and he yanked it over his head, dropping it over the side of the couch to join hers.

She traced her fingers through the dark hair that covered his chest. He hissed out a breath when she circled one flat nipple before tracing the tattoo along his ribs. "Is this a bulldog?"

He nodded. "Yeah. We had a bulldog named Lucy when Preston was a kid. She was the best dog."

"That's sweet." She kissed his neck and along his shoulder, trailing her tongue along his warm hard skin. "I want to see you naked."

"I want to taste your pussy," Hendrix said.

She blushed, but his straightforwardness was a massive turn-on for her. She studied him as he half sat up, propping himself on one arm. "If you're not comfortable with that, I -"

"No, no, I'm more than comfortable with that," she said quickly, making him grin. "But I owe you for -"

He shook his head before bending over and kissing just below her navel. "I don't keep score like that, Hazel."

"I don't either, but it doesn't seem fair that... oh God." She clutched at his head again when he licked a path above the waistband of her cotton pajama pants.

"That's you keeping score," he said. "Let me have a taste of your pussy, Hazel. I've been dreaming about it for weeks now."

"Well, in that case, have at it," she said.

He laughed and curled his fingers into the waistband of her pants. "Lift your hips."

She lifted her hips, grinning at the look on his face when

he pulled her pants down and discovered her lack of underwear.

"Fuck, woman, have you seriously been walking around here the whole night without panties?" he said.

"Seems like it," she said as he pulled her pants off and tossed them aside.

He stared at her pussy like a man starving, and, feeling sexy and powerful, she let her legs drop open, showing him her wet pussy. "You just gonna stare at it, handsome, or do something?"

His nostrils flared, and she squealed when he leaned in and nipped at her inner thigh. "Do something," he muttered. "Definitely do something."

That something turned out to be a long slow lick from her slit to the top of her clit. She cried his name, one hand digging into the couch, the other palming the back of his head and trying to push his face into her soaking wet pussy.

He grabbed her hand and pinned it to her thigh, grinning at her when she whined in complaint. "I want to take my time in tasting you, Hazel."

"I want you to go hard and fast," she said.

"Tell you what," he licked her clit again, that same slow and almost thoughtful taste that made her whole body shudder with pleasure, "I'll eat your pussy nice and slow, but fuck you hard and fast. Does that seem like a good compromise?"

"Oh God," she moaned when he sucked on her clit before licking her pussy lips. "I can't think... oh fuck, please, Hendrix."

"It's a good compromise," he murmured before burying his face in her pussy and – holy fuck – using his mouth and his lips to bring her almost instantly to her climax. She didn't know if it was a combination of it being such a long time since she'd had her pussy eaten or if Hendrix was some kind of pussy eating god, but when he sucked on her clit for the third time, she shrieked his name and came all over his face without a lick of embarrassment.

He made a muffled sound of surprise and pried her thighs apart before lifting his face and taking a deep breath.

"Whoops," she said breathlessly as the last of her climax washed over her. "Surprise…"

He laughed and snagged his t-shirt from the floor, wiping his face with it before kissing her inner thigh. "A happy surprise."

"Sorry, it's been a while since…" she motioned vaguely to her pussy and then his face.

"Well, now that's a real shame," he said before kissing her knee. "A pussy as delicious tasting as yours should be eaten daily."

"Such a sweet talker," she said. "Take off those pants and fuck me."

He laughed again, the sound making her feel warm and happier than her orgasm had. "You're not so much for the sweet-talking, I see."

"Not when I've wanted to see that glorious cock of yours for weeks," she said. "Don't be shy with me."

"Sweetheart, I don't have a shy bone in my body." He pulled his wallet out of his back pocket and handed her the condom he took from it. "Hold this."

She gripped it in one hand, watching with apt attention as Hendrix rose gracefully to his feet and unbuttoned his jeans. She tried not to drool when he dropped his jeans and briefs and freed his erect cock. Fuck, he was big and thick and positively delicious looking. She sat up and reached for him, wrapping her hand around the base and using her tongue to clean off the precum that slicked the fat head.

"Fuck," he groaned. His hands slid into her hair, and his hips thrust forward as she took more of him into her mouth. She sucked hard, relishing his salty taste as he smoothed her hair back and stared down at her with a hot and hungry gaze.

"Fuck, Hazel, keep sucking. Just like that... so good, honey. So good." His head fell back, and he moaned her name again before rocking his hips back and forth, meeting each slide of her mouth.

She sucked harder and faster, enjoying the soft grunts and groans he made with every bob of her head. When she pulled back and released him, his cry of protest made her smile.

She licked the head of his cock before holding out the condom. "Fuck me, Hendrix."

"Whatever you want, honey," he rasped before taking the condom from her with shaking hands.

He kicked off his jeans and briefs and tore open the package, rolling the condom on before kneeling between her legs.

"Wait," she said. "Do you want to go to the bedroom?"

"I can't wait that long," he said as he lined up his cock at her entrance.

"It's literally ten feet away," she said. "It'll take us two minutes to... oh! Oh God, Hendrix."

He had pushed into her with one smooth motion, and she clutched at his back when he dropped over her, propping himself up on his hands. "You okay?"

"Yeah, it's just... a lot. I need a minute to adjust."

He grinned, and she giggled at the smugness of it. "You're adorable when you're proud of your dick size."

"Thank you," he said, making her laugh again.

He sucked in a breath at her laugh and made a shallow thrust before his body went rigid. "Fuck. Sorry. You okay?"

"Yes." She slid her hands around his hips and hooked her

legs around his, resting her feet on the back of his calves. "It felt good. Let's try that again."

"Whatever you want," he groaned before making another couple of shallow thrusts.

"So good," she murmured. "Didn't you promise me hard and fast, though?"

His nostrils flared. "You sure, honey?"

"Positive," she said and squeezed around him. "Fuck me, Hendrix."

He moaned her name before thrusting in and out of her in a hard and rough rhythm that set her nerve endings ablaze. She met him stroke for stroke, their bodies growing slick with sweat. The only sounds in the room were the crackling fire, their soft grunts and groans, and the wet sound of her pussy taking his cock over and over again.

She shifted below him, crying out when it made the head of his cock rub against her g-spot. He stared down at her, the light of the fire washing over his face and revealing the sheer depth of his need for her. "So close, honey. I'm so fucking close."

"Me too," she panted. "Harder, Hendrix. Please."

He did what she asked, driving into her over and over, bouncing her on the couch as he stared with hungry desire at her breasts. She cupped them, pulling lightly on her hard and swollen nipples, and he shouted her name before his body stiffened, and he drove deep into her body.

She cried out, her orgasm washing over her as Hendrix made a few more hard and rapid thrusts before collapsing against her. Her body shaking, she kept her limbs wrapped around him, enjoying his heavy weight as his cock softened inside her.

"Holy fuck," he mumbled. "That was amazing."

"Hmm," she said, smiling at him when he lifted his head to study her. "It really was."

He smiled and pressed a kiss against her mouth before easing out of her and sitting up. "No regrets, Hazel?"

She sat up as well and cupped his face. "Not a single regret, Hendrix. I promise."

CHAPTER 13

Waking up in Hendrix's arms was the most peaceful Hazel had felt in years. She snuggled closer, smiling when Hendrix's arm tightened around her waist, and his hand cupping her breast squeezed gently.

"Morning, Hazel." He pressed a kiss against the back of her shoulder.

"Morning," she said. "Sounds like the storm has stopped."

"It has," he said. "Around two."

"You were still awake?" She had fallen asleep about two minutes after crawling into Hendrix's bed with him.

"I woke up a little after two to use the bathroom," he said.

She grabbed her phone from the nightstand. "Holy shit, it's almost eleven. Do you know how long it's been since I've slept in past eight?"

He chuckled. "You deserve a lazy morning in bed."

"I do," she agreed as she relaxed in Hendrix's arms. She tried sending a quick message to Spencer, frowning when it didn't go through. "Still no signal. I guess that means the power is still out."

"Not necessarily," Hendrix said. "We often don't get a signal even when the weather is good. It's one of the reasons I love this place. It forces me to unplug, so to speak."

She smiled before setting her phone down. "Do you think they've plowed the roads yet?"

"Doubtful," he said. "Why? Are you thinking about going somewhere?

His thumb rubbed over her nipple, and he pressed an open-mouthed kiss against her shoulder.

She smiled, rubbing her ass against Hendrix's morning wood. "No. Just wondered what the chances are of the boys arriving before I can fuck you again."

He plucked at her nipple. "Slim to none. Even if the roads are plowed, Preston knows what these roads are like after a snowstorm. He won't risk driving up here even this morning. In fact, they most likely won't make the drive at all this weekend."

"You're sure?" She arched her back when Hendrix pinched her nipple.

"Positive. So, why don't we -"

She wanted to die of embarrassment when her stomach grumbled so loudly it sounded like a damn truck driving through the bedroom.

"Shit, sorry," she said.

He laughed. "It's fine. C'mon, I'll make you something to eat.

"I'd rather have sex," she said.

"Your stomach disagrees." He grinned at her and kissed her forehead. "We'll check to see if the landline is working. If it is, you can call Spencer and let him know you're safe. He'll definitely be worried sick by now. Once you've talked to him, I'll make you some food, and we can spend the rest of the afternoon in bed. Deal?"

"Deal," she said.

"Do you know how incredible it is that not only do you cook, your food tastes amazing too?"

Hendrix laughed and finished rinsing the frying pan before handing it to Hazel to dry. "French toast isn't exactly cooking."

"It most definitely is. Especially when the power is out."

He laughed again. "You make it sound like I cooked the toast over an open flame instead of just turning on the generator."

She put her arms around him and kissed his chest through his t-shirt. "I'm being complimentary. Say thank you, Hendrix."

"Thank you, Hendrix," he said.

She giggled, and he smiled down at her before smoothing a strand of hair back from her face. He'd never seen Hazel like this before. Relaxed and a little silly, with no tension on her face. He'd do whatever he could to keep her like this.

He glanced at the landline as Hazel's hand wandered to his ass and squeezed. He wore thin pajama pants, and it was apparent how her touch affected him as his cock swelled and pressed against her stomach.

She gave him a sexy smile before kissing his chest. "Hi there."

"Hi." He caught her hand before she could slide it into his pants. "Why don't we recheck the landline."

"Sure." She crossed the kitchen and picked up the phone, holding it to her ear before setting it back in the cradle. "Still nothing."

She returned to him and slid her arms around his waist again. "Where were we?"

"I've got the four-wheel drive on the SUV, and if we drive half an hour down the mountain, we might have cell service. You could call Spencer and let him know you're okay."

"That's sweet but not necessary. I'll call him when the landline comes back."

"That may not happen until later tonight. Do you want Spencer to be worried all day about -"

"He won't be worried. Just trust me on this, okay? We don't have the same kind of relationship that you and Preston have. I promise you, if I thought Spencer was concerned, I'd do whatever was necessary to get a hold of him, but it's fine. He's having a good time with Preston, and," she traced her hand over his chest, "we're having a good time, right?"

"Yes," he said.

"Good. So, let's talk about how much I want to suck your dick again."

Any thought about trying to get a hold of the boys disappeared under a tidal wave of lust. His nostrils flaring, Hendrix pulled Hazel in close and palmed her ass. He bent his head and brushed his mouth over hers before flicking his tongue along her bottom lip. Her lips parted, and he slid his tongue into her mouth, taking the kiss deeper as she pressed her body against his and squeezed his ass.

He could kiss Hazel all day. She was so fucking sexy. He had no idea how he'd gotten so lucky that she wanted him, but he wasn't about to ask. He would just accept that he won the fucking lottery.

He gripped her hips and lifted her, setting her on the counter and crowding between her thighs. She giggled and put her arms around his shoulders, her cheeks flushed and her eyes sparkling. "I swear, I feel like a horny teenager right now."

"Me too," he said. "You ever had sex on a kitchen counter before?"

"Nope. You?"

"Never. But I've always wanted to."

"Well, today is your lucky day," she said.

He cupped her breast through her pajama top, circling her nipple with his thumb until it hardened and pressed against the thin fabric. She wrapped her legs around his waist, hooking her feet together at the small of his back as they kissed deeply. She rocked her pussy against him, and he moaned into her mouth.

"You keep doing that, and I really will fuck you right here on the counter. Food safety laws be damned," he said against her mouth.

She laughed and sucked hard on his lower lip. "If you don't fuck me on the counter, I'll be terribly disappointed."

"Is that right?" He pulled his shirt off and then yanked her shirt over her head and dropped both on the counter beside her before cupping her perfect tits and bending his head. "Well, I'd hate to disappoint you."

She moaned when he circled her nipples with his tongue before sucking on the right one. "That feels so good, Hendrix."

He slipped his hand inside her pants. "Are you wet for me, Haz -"

"What?" she asked when he lifted his head. "What's wrong?"

He stared at the front door with his head cocked as he listened intently. "Nothing," he said. "I thought I heard a door slam, but it's probably a branch cracking under the weight of the snow."

He kissed between her breasts, his fingers stroking the soft curls at the top of her mound. "Where were we?"

"You were about to fingerfuck me until I came on your fingers," Hazel said.

He grinned at her. "Is that right?"

"One hundred per -"

Hazel's voice died in her throat when the front door opened, and Preston and Spencer walked into the cabin on a blast of frigid air.

"I can't believe she drove up here. Mom, are you okay? Why did you drive to the cabin when... Mom?" Spencer stared in shock at them.

Hendrix immediately stepped closer to Hazel, pulling his hand out of her pants and shielding her naked upper body from the boys as Hazel's face paled and a low sound of dismay escaped her throat.

"Mom? What are you... what are you doing with Mr. Smith?"

"I think it's obvious what they're doing, Spence." Preston's face was full of glee, and he clapped his hands together. "Are you two dating?"

"Both of you turn around now," Hendrix said.

Preston immediately spun around at his tone, staring obediently at the door. Spencer continued to stare in disbelief at them, his eyes wide and his mouth open.

"Spencer!" Hendrix barked. "Turn around."

Spencer turned, groping for Preston's hand as Hendrix grabbed his and Hazel's shirts. He shrugged into his as a tight-lipped Hazel pulled hers over her head. She jumped down from the counter, pushing away from him and hurrying over to Spencer.

"You can turn around now, honey," Hazel said.

Hendrix frowned. "Hazel, you're not -"

She shook her head. "I'm leaving, Hendrix."

He watched in disbelief as she disappeared into the bedroom and returned only a minute later, still in her pajamas with her suitcase in her hand. She pulled her coat on and shoved her bare feet into her boots as she grabbed her purse from the table.

"Hazel, you can't go," Hendrix said. "The roads are still bad."

"He's right," Preston said. "They're plowed, but they're icy. You should stay, Hazel."

Hazel hesitated, staring at Spencer, who refused to look at her. His whole body trembled, and he looked like he was on the verge of throwing up. "Either you leave, or I leave, Mom."

"Jesus Christ," Hendrix said. "Stop being a selfish little brat and -"

"Hendrix, enough!" Hazel glared at him. "Don't say another word."

She turned to Spencer. "I'll leave. Stay here where it's safe. I know you're angry with me, but please call me when you return to the city, and I'll explain everything."

Spencer looked away, his lips tightening and his hand holding Preston's so tightly his knuckles were white.

"Hazel," Preston said. "Please stay."

"I'll text you when I get home, so you know I'm safe," Hazel said.

"Whatever," Spencer said.

"Spencer!" Preston stared at him in shock.

Hazel touched Preston's shoulder. "Spencer needs you, honey. Okay?"

Preston studied Spencer's pale face and nodded. "Yeah, okay."

Without looking at Hendrix, Hazel opened the door and stepped outside, shutting it behind her.

There was silence for a few seconds before Preston said, "Dad?"

"Fuck!" Hendrix turned and stalked to his bedroom, slamming the door shut.

CHAPTER 14

"You still haven't heard from Spencer, huh?" Indie sank onto the couch beside Sierra, blowing on the mug of hot tea she held before taking a sip.

"Not yet." Hazel stared listlessly at her tea mug.

"Have you talked to Hendrix?" Indie asked.

"Yes, on the phone. He called me Monday as soon as he returned to the city. He wanted to come over, but I told him it wasn't a good idea and that it was best if we didn't see each other outside of events with Preston and Spencer."

She laughed bitterly. "Which was pointless because Spencer will never let me spend time with him and Preston again. Hell, he'll probably never talk to me again."

"It's only been three days," Sierra said, "and Spencer is a lot like his dad. Garrett used to give you the silent treatment for weeks if you pissed him off. Once Spencer cools down, he'll talk to you about what happened."

"I'm not sure that he will," Hazel said. "He loves Preston, and he really likes Hendrix, and now I've put his relationship with the both of them in jeopardy."

"That," Sierra said, "is complete fucking bullshit."

"Sierra," Indie said.

"What?"

"We agreed we'd be supportive," she said.

"I am being supportive," Sierra said.

"And we'd be kind," Indie said.

"Fuck kind," Sierra said. "It's time to be blunt. You are not to blame for this, Hazel."

Hazel stared at Sierra. "Did you forget the part where Spencer and Preston walked in on Hendrix and me while we were half-naked?"

"So fucking what?" Sierra said. "You're allowed to get naked with a guy."

"I'm pretty sure there's a rule about getting naked with my son's boyfriend's father," Hazel said.

"There isn't," Indie said. "I checked."

Sierra laughed as Hazel gave her a look. "You did not, Indie."

"You didn't do anything wrong," Sierra said.

"Spencer hates me again," Hazel said miserably. "All of the therapy, all of the work I've done to show Spencer that I'm not who I used to be, and I destroy it in a moment because I'm fucking horny!"

She slammed her free hand down on the chair arm. "Ow, shit." She shook her hand as pain throbbed up the side of it.

"Hazel, honey, you need to listen to me," Sierra said.

"Sierra," Indie said, "maybe this isn't the right time."

"It's the perfect time. We agreed on the drive over we were doing this," Sierra said.

"Doing what?" Hazel said.

"Being honest with you."

"You've been lying to me?" Hazel said.

Sierra's sharp glare made Hazel feel almost sorry for the criminals in her courtroom at the receiving end of that glare.

"You know we haven't been lying to you. By being honest, I mean that we tell you it's time you stopped living for Spencer and started living for yourself."

Hazel's mouth dropped open, and she set her mug on the end table beside the chair. "Are you serious right now, Sierra?"

"I am, and Indie agrees with me. Don't you, Indie?"

Indie looked a little sick to her stomach, but she nodded. "Yes, I do."

"How can you say that? It's exactly what I've been doing since Spencer moved out," Hazel said. "I've worked so hard to show Spencer that I won't smother him and that I'm my own person and -"

"Yes, you have, babe," Sierra said, "and we are so fucking proud of you. You have no idea how proud we are." She crossed the room and crouched in front of Hazel, staring solemnly at her. "There isn't a day that goes by where I'm not amazed by how incredibly strong you are. You faced harsh truths about yourself without any self-pity and have worked hard every day to be the person you want to be."

She took Hazel's hands and squeezed them. "We are so proud of you for how far you've come. But you're still living for Spencer."

"I'm not," Hazel said. "I'm living for me and -"

Sierra reached up and tapped her gently on the forehead. "In here, you're living for you, but in here," she touched Hazel's chest directly over her heart, "you're still living for Spencer."

Hazel stared blankly at her. "I... I don't...."

Indie joined them and sat on the arm of the chair, putting her arm around Hazel's shoulders. "You are, honey. I want you to answer a question for me. Don't think about it. Just answer with the first reply that comes into your head. Besides

Spencer talking to you again, what do you want most at this moment?"

"To be with Hendrix," Hazel said.

"Then be with him," Sierra said.

"It will destroy my relationship with Spencer," Hazel said as her stomach rolled and the throbbing pain behind her right eye intensified.

"Spencer will get over it, and if he doesn't, that's on him," Indie said.

Hazel stared in surprise at her. She was used to Sierra's bluntness, but hearing Indie like that was shocking.

Indie stared solemnly at her. "I love you, Hazel, both of us do, and we want you to be happy. Having a relationship with Spencer makes you happy, but so does being with Hendrix. You know how much we love your kid. He's good, and he's kind, but he doesn't always extend that kindness to you."

"Because I -"

"Because you weren't perfect," Sierra said. "Well, news-fucking-flash, no parent is. We love our kids, and we try our best, and when we fuck up, we say sorry and try to do better in the future. That's what being a good parent is, and that's what you are, Hazel. Spencer is using your mistakes as a weapon against you, and it has to stop. You are allowed to live your life without always considering Spencer. He's your kid, but he's not your keeper."

"I don't want to hurt him again."

Sierra shrugged. "No parent wants to hurt their kid, but it doesn't mean you have to give up what you want to make him happy. Would Spencer give up Preston to make you happy?"

"Of course not, and he shouldn't," Hazel said.

"So, why are you?" Indie said.

Hazel stared silently at her, her brain too busy processing what her friends were saying to attempt an answer that wasn't straight up gobblygook.

"Why do you want to be with Hendrix?" Sierra asked.

"Well, because he's smart and sexy and thoughtful. He makes me feel good when I'm with him, and not just because of the sex, you know? I like who I am when I'm with him. Plus, he adores his kid, and he's an amazing dad."

"And none of those reasons have anything to do with your kid," Sierra said. "If you want to show Spencer that you value yourself and aren't just living for him, then being with Hendrix is a surefire way to get that message across."

"He won't believe me," Hazel said. "I tried to tell him it had nothing to do with him, and he refused to believe it."

"He was in shock over walking in on you and Hendrix about to bang," Sierra said. "He's had a few days to absorb it. Talk to him again."

"And if he still won't believe it?" Hazel said.

Indie squeezed her shoulders. "That's not your problem, honey."

"I don't want to destroy his relationship with Preston."

"I don't think you dating Hendrix will do that," Sierra said. "Preston and Spencer have been together for a while, and it's easy to see how much they love each other. Spencer should want that kind of happiness for you too, babe. Spencer's a good kid who loves you. He'll come around when he sees how happy you are with Hendrix."

"Agreed," Indie said.

"I deserve to be happy, too," Hazel said slowly.

"Yes, you do." Sierra stared up at her. "You really do."

"I hurt Hendrix when I said we couldn't be together. When I chose Spencer over him,"

"If Hendrix is as good of a guy as you say he is, then he'll understand when you apologize and ask for a second chance," Sierra said. "Throw in a blowjob with the apology, and you'll be golden."

"Sierra!" Indie said.

"What?" Sierra said. "I'm not saying *every* problem can be solved with a well-timed blowjob, but they certainly can be helpful in the right situation."

"Oh my God," Indie said.

"You know I'm right." Sierra grinned at Hazel before standing and pulling her to her feet. "You've got this, babe." She slapped her on the ass and pushed her toward the door. "Go talk to your kid, and then head to Hendrix's place and enjoy some hot make-up sex."

———

"HAZEL!" PRESTON THREW HIS ARMS AROUND HER AND hugged her hard. "I'm so happy to see you."

"I'm happy to see you too, honey." She kissed his cheek and stepped back, smiling at him. "I'm so sorry about Saturday and -"

"Stop. You don't have to apologize," Preston said. "I'm glad you and my dad were, uh… dating for a bit."

"Are you doing okay?" she said.

"Fine. Are you? Dad said he talked to you Monday night, and you were pretty upset."

"I'm all right. How are things with you and Spencer?"

"Fine," he said.

Relief washed over her, making her feel a little weak. "You're sure?"

"Positive." Preston took her hand, his face turning a little red. "As much as I keep pretending you're my mom like I'm some dumb little kid, I love Spencer, and I'm always going to be on his side."

He paused, staring blankly at her. "Shit, was that rude? That came out rude, didn't it?"

She laughed. "No, it's fine. I appreciate your honesty, and you loving Spencer and always being there for him is what I want most."

He smiled, and she took his hand and squeezed it. "But I'm also glad you think of me as a mom, Preston. I love you, honey."

"I love you too, Hazel."

"Is Spencer home?"

"Yeah. He's in the office. My dad came by just before supper and talked with Spencer, and they smoothed things over between them."

"Good," she said as more relief poured through her. "That's good. I want Spencer and your dad to have a good relationship."

Preston glanced behind him before lowering his voice. "Spencer won't admit this, but he's looking for a father figure as much as I'm looking for a mother. He wants my dad to like him."

"I think Hendrix is good for Spencer, and I'm glad they talked," Hazel said.

"My dad said you ended it with him," Preston said. "I don't suppose I could convince you to give him another chance, huh? I know Spence has a problem with it, but, um, you don't have to tell him, right?"

She squeezed his hand again. "I won't lie to Spencer, but after I speak with him, I plan to head over to your dad's and ask him for a second chance."

Preston's face lit up, and he hugged her again, his thin body thrumming with excitement. "Seriously? That's awesome! Dad won't admit it, but he's miserable without you, and I hate seeing him that way. He deserves to be happy. He deserves someone as awesome as you. Hell, I won't even care how weird it'll be when you two get married, and Spencer and I are technically stepbrothers."

"Whoa," Hazel said with a smile. "No one's getting married. Your dad might not even want to date me."

"He will," Preston said confidently.

She hoped he was right, but she couldn't think about Hendrix right now. She was here to talk to Spencer, and she needed every ounce of energy and concentration to make sure she didn't fuck it up. "I'm going to go talk to Spencer."

"Okay." Preston kissed her cheek. "Good luck."

"Thanks, honey." She walked down the short hallway to the office. She knocked on the closed door, opening it at Spencer's 'come in'.

He sat at the desk, staring blankly out the window at the falling snow. She stepped inside and closed the door. "Hi, Spence."

He jumped, his hands clenching together as he stared at her. "What are you doing here?"

"I came to talk to you."

"I don't feel like talking."

"I know you don't, but you've avoided me long enough," Hazel said.

"Have I?" he said. "Because I didn't realize there was a time limit to how long a person could avoid their mother after he caught her having sex with his boyfriend's father."

She straightened her back and stared steadily at him. "I understand how traumatic it was for you to find out Hendrix and I were involved that way, and I'm sorry for that. But I won't apologize for having wants and needs or for being attracted to Hendrix."

"He's Preston's dad," Spencer said. "Did you even think about that for a minute, or are you too selfish to -"

"Stop it," she said sharply. "I may be many things, but selfish isn't one of them, and you know damn well I'm not."

He looked away, his face red and his eyes overbright. Hazel hated upsetting him, but he needed to hear what she had to say. "Spencer, look at me."

He turned his gaze to hers, and she said, "I will only say this once – I was attracted to Hendrix and planned on asking him out before I knew he was Preston's father. He came into my shop, and we had an immediate connection. Two days later, he returned to the store and asked me out on a date. We made plans for Friday night. When I showed up for dinner on Thursday night and realized who Hendrix was, I cancelled our date and told him we couldn't see each other."

"So, why were you with him at the cabin? Why did you have sex with him?" Spencer said.

"I'm sure you already know this, but I left early and got caught in the snowstorm. The storm was terrible when I got to the cabin, and I couldn't drive home. I had sex with Hendrix because I am an adult who is attracted to another adult, and I am allowed to sleep with whomever I want."

"Even when it's my boyfriend's father," Spencer said bitterly.

"I'll admit that's not ideal, but it happened, and we have to deal with it. I like Hendrix a lot, and I -"

"You can't date him," Spencer said. "I won't allow it."

His face flushed bright red when she laughed. "Kid, I love you, but just like I don't have the right to tell you what to do, you don't have that right with me. I will consider your feelings, always, but I'm also going to live my life."

"So, that means what? You're going to date Hendrix?"

"Yes. If he'll give me a second chance."

Spencer stood and walked to the window, staring out at the snow. "What if I said I'll cut off contact with you if you date him?"

Her stomach dropped, but she took a calming breath and joined him at the window. "Don't do that, Spencer. Don't be manipulative. It isn't who you are."

His face went red, and he looked over at her. "I'm sorry."

"I want to clarify that my reasons for dating Hendrix have nothing to do with you. I want to date him because he's smart, kind, and funny, and I like how he makes me feel. He's a good dad who loves his kid *and* the person his kid is dating."

Spencer's bottom lip trembled, and he took a deep breath. "I don't want to ruin your chance at happiness, but I don't want to be...."

"Smothered," she finished. "I know that, honey. Will we spend more time together if Hendrix and I date? Probably. But that doesn't mean I won't continue to respect your boundaries. I will. But I need you to do something for me."

"What's that?" he asked.

"Recognize that I'm human and I make mistakes. I'm not perfect, and I'll probably still make mistakes when it comes to being your mother, but I love you."

"I love you too." A tear slid down Spencer's cheek.

She reached out and rubbed it away with her thumb. "Look at me, honey."

He turned to face her, and she cupped his face in her hands. "I love you, Spencer. You mean the world to me, but you are not my *whole* world. Okay?"

He nodded and let her wipe away the fresh tears on his cheeks. "Okay. Can I ask you a question?"

"Of course," she said.

"You never smothered Dad, did you?"

"No," she said evenly. "I didn't."

He sighed, and the guilt that crossed his face made her heart ache fiercely for him. "It's okay, honey."

"It isn't," he said. "When I first moved out to live with Grandma and Grandpa, I would have dinner with Dad sometimes, and I... I complained about you. I told him how much you were always hovering over me, and he said that you did it to him too. That it was the reason he left you, and you deserved to be alone. I agreed with him."

His voice broke, and Hazel hugged him hard, rubbing his back. "Don't cry, Spence."

"Complaining about you was the first time Dad ever really paid attention to me, and I thought it meant that he loved me."

"He does love you, honey," Hazel said.

"No, he doesn't. Not like you do." Spencer scrubbed at his face. "There was a part of me that knew he was lying, but I refused to admit it. I'm sorry."

"It's in the past," she said. "You and I are both different people now."

"We are," he said. "And I promise I'll be better, that I'll try hard every day to see you for who you are now."

"I know you will, Spence." She kissed his forehead. "I'm headed over to Hendrix's now. I'll text you in a few days, and if you're up to it, we'll have coffee. I love you."

"I love you too."

She headed for the door, pausing in the doorway when Spencer said, "Mom?"

"Yeah?"

"I'm sorry I've been an asshole. You're a good mom."

She brushed away the hot tears that flowed down her cheeks. "Thank you, honey."

CHAPTER 15

Hendrix opened the fridge, looked inside, and then closed the door. He stared blankly at the calendar on the refrigerator before opening the door again.

He needed to eat something, but he had no appetite. It was why he'd turned down Preston's offer to eat dinner with them. He didn't need his kid knowing he was so upset he couldn't eat.

I think he already knows how upset you are.

Wasn't that the fucking truth. And what did it say about Hendrix's level of emotional attachment to Hazel, that no longer seeing her upset him to the point that even Preston could see it? Not that Preston didn't care about him, but Hendrix had always done a fine job hiding his emotions from his kid. But this…

Was different.

He closed the fridge and left the kitchen, sinking onto the living room couch and staring at the television. He'd turned it on when he got home, but it was for noise and nothing else. The house felt too empty and quiet tonight, and he'd hoped the television would drown out his inner thoughts.

While he was thankful he and Spencer had talked and eased the tension between them, Hendrix was fooling himself if he didn't think he was holding onto a bit of resentment toward Spencer for ruining any chance of dating Hazel. Which he needed to figure out how to let go of because Preston loved Spencer a great deal and nothing was more important to Hendrix than Preston's happiness.

Not even your own?

He stared morosely at the television. Did it even matter? Hazel wouldn't date him even if –

The doorbell made him jump like a scared little kid. He glanced at his phone. It was after eight, and it had been snowing steadily since he left work at four. Who would be out in weather like this?

He stood and shut off the television before walking to the door and opening it. A surprised "ungh" escaped his mouth as he stared at Hazel standing on the front porch. She was bundled up in a thick coat with a scarf wrapped around her throat and bright blue mittens on her hands, but snowflakes clung to her dark hair, and her cheeks were red.

"Hazel? What are you doing here?" he said.

"I wanted to talk with you," she said. "I'm sorry I didn't text first."

"That's fine. What, uh, what's going on?"

"Do you think we could talk inside? It's freezing out here," she said.

"Shit, yes. Of course. Sorry, come in." Blushing at his stupidity, he stepped back, and Hazel stepped inside.

She closed the door and took off her jacket, mittens, and scarf. She toed off her boots as he hung her jacket in the closet. He tried not to stare at her amazing breasts in the tight-fitting sweater she wore.

146

"Come into the kitchen. Do you want some coffee?"

She followed him into the kitchen. "Do you have tea? If I drink coffee now, I'll be up all night."

"I have tea," he said. "Sit down."

She sat, and he quickly made them two cups of tea and placed milk and sugar on the table. He sat beside her, watching as she stirred in sugar and milk before sipping the tea. "Thank you. It's good."

"You're welcome."

They sat silently for almost ten seconds before he said, "The roads are terrible tonight."

"They are," she agreed. "Not driving up a mountain in a snowstorm bad, but bad enough."

More silence descended, and he cracked his knuckles. "Hazel, why are -"

"Hendrix, I'm sorry -"

They both stopped, and Hendrix said, "You first."

She took a deep breath. "I'm sorry for misleading you Monday night when we talked."

He frowned. "What do you mean?"

"I told you the only thing that mattered to me was Spencer's happiness. That isn't true. I mean, it's important to me because I love Spencer, but my happiness needs to be important to me too. Don't you think?"

"Yes," he said. He didn't want that stupid hope building in his chest, but there it was, setting up shop and refusing to leave.

"Anyway, I told myself we couldn't date because it would upset Spencer, and if I were a good mom, I wouldn't do something that deliberately upset my kid. But then I realized that not dating you upset me a great deal, and how can I be a good mom when I'm not happy?"

"Hazel," he said, "are you -"

"I can't be a good mom, a good employer, a good friend when I'm miserable, Hendrix." She leaned forward and took his hands, rubbing her thumb across his knuckles. "And I am miserable without you."

"Me too," he said.

She stared solemnly at him. "I have spent so much time and energy the last few years trying to make Spencer see that I'm not who I used to be. That I wasn't a helicopter mom anymore, I had my own wants and needs, and my world didn't revolve around him. I thought I'd made progress and, you know what? I have made some. But I've realized if I give up what I want now, if I don't date you, then inside here," she tapped her chest, "I'm still the same person I was. My world is still wrapped completely around Spencer's, and that isn't healthy for him, but more importantly, it isn't healthy for me."

She stared at their clasped hands. "I deserve to be happy, Hendrix. What makes me happy is being with you. Would you give us another chance? Forget everything I said Monday night and start fresh? I promise I -"

"Yes," he said. "Hell, yes."

She blinked at him before a wide grin spread across her face. "Yeah?"

"Yeah," he said before leaning forward and kissing her.

She returned his kiss, cupping his face and brushing her mouth across his, slowly and softly. When she nipped his bottom lip, he groaned and broke the kiss, resting his forehead against hers. "Hazel, I am definitely in for dating, but what if Spencer cuts you out of his life because of it? I won't be the reason your son won't talk to you or -"

"I've already spoken to Spencer," Hazel said. "I stopped at his and Preston's place before I came here. I won't say he's thrilled I planned on asking you to date me because he isn't. There's a chance the next few months will be rough while Spencer realizes I meant what I said about our relationship having nothing to do with him, but being with you is worth it to me."

She leaned back a little, her hands still cupping his face. "Of course, I'll understand if it isn't worth it to you. It may strain things with Preston, he's fully team Spencer as he should be, and I will not ask you to risk your and Preston's relationship for me. Preston needs you in his life and needs to know you're always on his side."

He loved how concerned she was about Preston. "I think it'll be okay. Preston and I have a pretty solid relationship, and I'm certain he'll be over the moon about the two of us dating."

An adorable smile crept across Hazel's face. "He was pretty happy when I told him I was talking to you tonight."

"See?" He reached over, wrapped his arms around Hazel's waist and hauled her up and into his lap. "I knew he'd be happy about it. He loves you."

"I love him too. And I think Spencer will be happy for us after a period of adjustment."

"I think so too. He's a good kid," Hendrix said.

She smoothed her hand through his hair. The soft weight of her on his lap felt perfect and unbelievably right. "He is. Thank you for talking to him tonight, Hendrix. Preston told me you stopped by to smooth things over with him. It means a great deal to me that you didn't blame him for my decision."

He pressed a kiss against the hollow of her throat. "I like Spencer, and I know how much he loves Preston and how much Preston loves him. I want the two of them to be happy."

"I want that too. But," she traced her thumb over his bottom lip, "I want us to be happy as well."

She kissed him again and made a soft sound of need when he hardened against her ass. She tugged his head back and stared down at him. "Do you know what would make me very happy right now, Hendrix?"

"What's that?" he asked.

"Riding you in your bed."

He stood up so fast she nearly fell on her ass. He caught her and pulled her up against him, loving her breathless little laugh and the way she ground against his hard dick. "Hmm… you seem to be into that idea as well."

"I want you so much, I can't even try to be cool about it," Hendrix said as he led her to his bedroom. "Do you know how many times I've nearly been electrocuted this week because the image of your naked body and the memory of how tight your pussy was around my dick kept popping into my head while I was working?"

He loved how she blushed as he tugged at the hem of her sweater. He pulled it over her head, and she grinned up at him. "Yesterday, it took me three tries to balance the till. Eventually, Carlos just took it from me and did it themselves. I might have been distracted by certain thoughts myself."

"I'm glad I wasn't the only one distracted." He yanked his shirt over his head and dropped it on the floor as she shimmied out of her jeans and gracefully tugged off her socks.

"You weren't," she said as she unbuckled his belt and pulled it open before unbuttoning his jeans. "But at least with my job, there's no danger of me dying because I can't stop thinking about your dick."

He laughed and shoved his jeans down his legs. They took his briefs with him, and Hazel made a soft sound of need when his cock sprung free, the head of it already leaking precum. She reached for his dick, wrapping her soft hand around the shaft as he reached behind her and unhooked her bra.

"Fuck," he groaned when she stroked him firmly. "That feels so good, sweetheart."

He raked her bra down her arms, and she let him go long enough to allow the straps to slide past her hands before gripping him again. "I've missed being with you, Hendrix."

He tossed her bra on the floor and cupped her tits, rubbing his thumbs over her nipples until they hardened. "I've missed that too."

He slid his arms around her waist and pulled her up against him, dropping a kiss against her mouth. "It wasn't just the sex I missed, Hazel. I want you to know that."

She smiled at him. "Same for me."

He kissed her again, sliding his tongue into her mouth and brushing it along hers as she moaned, and her hand tightened around his aching cock. When they came up for air, she said, "But I also really missed the sex."

He backed up, bringing her with him until his legs hit the bed. "Same, girl."

She laughed and gave him a gentle push, making him fall back on the bed before she straddled him and leaned over, propping herself up on her hands on the bed as her breasts brushed enticingly against his chest.

He cupped her breasts, gently squeezing them as he played with her nipples. She rubbed her pussy against him, the silky softness of her panties teasing his dick.

"Why are you wearing underwear?" he said.

She shrugged. "Someone didn't take them off me. Slacker."

He laughed and kissed her collarbone. "Stand up for a minute."

She climbed off and stood beside the bed, facing him as he sat up, his legs dangling over the bed. He pulled her between his legs and kissed between her breasts before kissing his way to one rosy nipple and sucking it into his mouth. He sucked hard, enjoying how she gasped and moaned as he teased her other nipple with his thumb and finger. He released her nipple with a soft pop and stared up at her.

"You are so fucking sexy, Hazel."

"So are you," she said as her fingers dug into his shoulders. "I'm so wet already."

"I should probably check for myself," he said with a grin.

"Fantastic idea," she moaned as his fingers traced tiny circles down her flat abdomen to the waistband of her panties.

Part of him wanted to tease her and make her need him so much that she was begging for his cock, but he couldn't wait. Not tonight. He needed to see her, taste her, be inside of her.

He hooked his fingers in the waistband and tugged her panties down her thighs. His mouth watered, and he lost all interest in removing her panties when her gorgeous pussy was revealed. He leaned forward and kissed the soft curls at the top of her mound. She moaned and shoved her panties down, stepping out of them as he hooked one hand around her firm thigh.

"Lift your leg, sweetheart."

She lifted her leg, resting her foot on the bed as he reached between her legs and traced her inner thigh. She moaned, and her pelvis rocked forward, her hand clutching his head when he kissed below her belly button.

"Hendrix, please," she said.

He cupped her pussy, his cock growing even harder at how wet she was. He rubbed her clit with his thumb and slid one finger into her tightness, a groan escaping his throat when she squeezed around his finger.

"Condom," she said breathlessly as she rocked against his hand. "Where are they?"

"In the nightstand drawer, but I want to taste you again."

She cried out when he rubbed her clit again and shook her head. "I want that too, but later, please? I can't wait, Hendrix. I need you. I need to fuck you again. The ache... I can't stand it. Hendrix, please."

Despite how much he wanted his face buried in her sweet tasting pussy again, he pressed another soft kiss against her stomach and pulled his hand away. "Whatever you want, sweetheart."

She moved a couple of steps to the nightstand and opened the drawer, pulling out the condom and ripping the foil. "Still good with me being on top?"

"Hell, yes," he said as he rearranged his body on the bed until he was lying on his back with a pillow propped under his head. He patted his stomach. "Climb on, sweetheart."

She grinned and straddled his thighs before carefully rolling the condom over his dick. She fumbled with it and said, "Sorry, it's been a while since I've done this."

He gritted his teeth at the feel of her soft hand. "You're doing great."

She laughed and knee-walked her way up the bed until her pussy rubbed against his cock. He moaned out another curse, his hands clenching around her thighs. "Hazel, I need your pussy, right now."

She gripped the base of his dick, holding him steady as she lowered herself down. He moaned her name, forcing himself not to buck up as her pussy took him inch by agonizing inch.

"So good," she breathed when she took the last of him,

her ass sitting snugly on him and his cock buried in her hot, wet pussy.

"Yes," he groaned. "Fuck me, Hazel."

"Hmm," she said before bracing her hands on his chest and letting her head fall back. She rode him with long, slow strokes, taking him from root to tip as he rubbed her smooth thighs and stared at her gorgeous breasts.

When she cupped them and played with her nipples, he grunted out a curse and gripped her hips, holding her tight as he thrust into her over and over. She cried his name, her knees squeezing into his hips as she rode his thrusts, her fingers tugging and pulling on her nipples.

"Oh God," she moaned. "Right there, Hendrix. Right there... don't stop, keep...."

He reached for her clit, but she made a sharp cry of pleasure, and her pussy squeezed tight around his dick as her orgasm washed over her. She bounced on his dick, her hands squeezing her breasts, her face beautiful in the aftermath of her climax.

He thrust harder, staring at her as his balls tightened and his need for her overwhelmed him. He cried her name as he came inside her, pulling her down against him and wrapping his arms around her waist as he pumped in and out of her. Her breath panted in his ear, her nipples were hard pearls against his chest, and she made a soft sound of pleasure when he made a final thrust before collapsing on the bed.

She tried to sit up, and he tightened his arms around her. "No, not yet, sweetheart."

She relaxed against him, lightly running her fingers up and down his arm as their breathing slowed and the sweat dried on their bodies.

When she wiggled against him, he reluctantly let her go, smoothing his hand over her ass as she climbed off him and collapsed on the bed. He removed the condom and threw it in the trash can next to the nightstand before pulling up the covers as Hazel snuggled against him.

"Thank you for the orgasm, Hendrix," she said.

He laughed. "You're welcome. Thank you for making me come so hard I saw stars."

She giggled before running her hand over his chest, fingers toying with the dark hair covering it. After a minute or so, she said, "It's getting late."

He automatically tightened his hold on her. He knew it was too soon to ask Hazel to spend the night, but after sharing a bed with her at the cabin, he wanted her in his arms all night again.

"The weather is pretty bad," he said.

"It is," she agreed.

"Probably too dangerous to drive."

She sat up and smiled at him. "Are you asking me to stay for a sleepover, Hendrix?"

"I am," he said.

"I have to work in the morning," she said.

"So do I."

Her smile widened. "It is snowing a lot."

"It's definitely not safe for you to drive home," he said.

"We'll have to get up extra early so I can drive home to shower and change before work," she said.

"What's this 'we' business?" he said.

She laughed and poked him in the ribs. "If I have to get up early because of your sleepover, so do you."

"Worth it." He cupped her face, rubbing his thumb over her cheekbone. "Stay the night with me. I like having you in my bed."

"I like it too." She kissed his palm. "I'd love to have a sleepover with you."

Happiness washed over him, and he pulled her back into his arms, kissing her temple as she cuddled up to him. "I'm happy you're here with me, Hazel."

She smiled at him and then kissed his chest. "Me too, Hendrix."

EPILOGUE

"You know, for someone who owns a flower shop, you have very little 'girl' stuff."

Hazel raised her eyebrows at Hendrix. "Girl stuff?"

"You know," he gestured vaguely at the bookshelf they'd just finished filling. "Knickknacks and tchotchkes and shit. We put nothing but books on this bookshelf."

She laughed and wrapped her arms around his waist. "One, knickknacks doesn't equate to girl stuff, two, owning a flower shop doesn't automatically mean I'm into girl stuff, and three – I'd rather have a bookshelf full of books over tchotchkes any day."

He kissed her forehead even though she was sweaty and gross and probably smelled worse than a teenage boy. "I want to be certain you didn't toss things you wanted to keep. This is your house now too, Hazel. I want you to be surrounded by things that make you happy."

She squeezed his waist. "I didn't get rid of anything I wanted, honey. I promise. It felt good to purge so much stuff, and besides, you purged a bunch, too, so there would be room for the stuff I kept. It was a mutual purging."

He kissed her forehead a second time. "Do you know when I realized how much Preston loves you?"

"When was that?" she said.

"When I told him I wanted to clean out his childhood bedroom and turn it into an office for you. He didn't blink an eye. Just said sure and asked when I wanted him to come by and help clean it. He's always been weirdly attached to his room, but he wants you to be happy here."

Warmth washed over Hazel. "He's such a good kid. I love him."

"I know you do. Which, thank God, because I think the number of daily texts from him has actually increased over the last six months."

"I don't mind," Hazel said as she studied the room. "Although you insisting I have an office at home when I have a perfectly good one at the store is a little much."

"Your office at the store is a tiny closet in the back room with barely enough room for you to sit," Hendrix said. "Also, we agreed that you needed to spend less time at the shop. Having the office here means you can work from home on the days you need to do your bookkeeping and other office-related items."

"We agreed?" Hazel said. "Don't you mean Carlos and you?"

"And Ruby," Hendrix said.

Hazel laughed. "I'm pretty sure you were the one who told Ruby and Carlos to threaten to quit if I didn't take one day off a week."

"Nope, they came up with that diabolical plot twist all on their own," Hendrix said. "I was so proud of them."

"One of my regulars at the store thought living together after six months of dating was moving too fast," Hazel said.

"Wait until they find out I asked you to marry me," Hendrix said.

Hazel grinned. "We really need to tell the boys."

"We will," Hendrix said. "As soon as the engagement ring is resized. We can't announce we're getting married without a ring on your finger."

"I don't think that's an actual engagement rule," Hazel said.

"It is for me." Hendrix gave her a thoughtful look. "Do you think we're moving too fast?"

"No, do you?"

"No. Which is all that matters, right?"

She smiled. "Yes. I love you, Hendrix."

"I love you too. Now, what do you say we celebrate the unpacking of the final box," Hendrix pointed to the empty box sitting near the bookshelf, "with some pussy eating and 'scream until the neighbours make a noise complaint' sex?"

"Totally," Hazel said. "But after we both shower."

"Are you saying I smell?" Hendrix asked.

"We've been unpacking boxes and rearranging furniture all day," she said. "We both smell."

"Harsh but fair." Hendrix squeezed her ass before kissing her. "Let's get in the shower."

The front door opened, and she heard Spencer say, "Remind me to ask Mom about the casserole recipe," before Preston's voice echoed down the hall.

"Hey, Dad! Where are you guys?"

"In the office," Hendrix called.

Hazel thought he did well at masking the disappointment in his voice, but his face... that was a different story.

She tugged his head down to hers and whispered in his ear, "After the boys leave, I'll suck your dick in the shower."

His nostrils flared, and he squeezed her ass again. "You are killing me, woman."

She laughed and kissed his chest through his t-shirt.

"Wait… are you decent?" Spencer hollered, making Preston laugh.

"Oh my God, Spence, get over it. It's not like they spend all their time banging each other," Preston said.

"That's what he thinks," Hendrix muttered.

Hazel laughed again as the boys walked into the room.

"Holy shit," Preston said. "It looks great in here."

Hazel untangled herself from Hendrix. "Thank you again for letting me use your room as an office, Preston."

Preston grinned at her. "It's your house now too, Hazel. You deserve to have an office." He went to embrace her, and she took a step back.

"You might want to hold off on the hugging. I've been unpacking boxes all day, and I'm sweaty and smell."

"Don't care," Preston said before hugging her.

She returned his hug and smiled at Spencer when Preston walked over to Hendrix and hugged him. 'Hi, honey. How are you?"

"Good. The house looks great. Sorry I couldn't come by today to help you finish unpacking," Spencer said.

"That's fine. You and Preston did so much with the move already. I can't thank you enough."

Spencer grinned at her. His body was nearly vibrating, and a weird expression of excitement and nerves crossed his face. "So, um, Preston and I have some news."

Preston brushed by her and took Spencer's hand. Now they both looked nervous and excited, and she glanced at Hendrix when he joined her. He took her hand and shrugged slightly before saying, "What's up, guys?"

They smiled at each other before Preston said, "I asked Spencer to marry me, and he said yes."

"Oh my God!" Hazel said. "You're getting married?"

"Yes." Spencer showed her his left hand, where a platinum band with a row of three small diamonds sat on his ring finger.

"Holy shit," Hendrix said. "That's awesome. Congratulations, guys."

"You're getting married," Hazel repeated. Trying not to cry, she pulled Spencer in for a tight hug, not caring that she was sweaty and gross. "Oh, honey. I am so happy for you both."

"Thanks, Mom." Spencer hugged her hard before grinning at her. "You're pretty surprised, huh?"

"Yes," she said, "but I shouldn't be because the two of you are perfect for each other."

She didn't want to cry, but she couldn't help it. She swiped at the tears as Preston threw his arms around her. She returned his hug, watching happily as Hendrix shook Spencer's hand before hugging him.

"We're really happy for you guys," Hendrix said.

Preston slung his arm around Hazel's shoulders, smiling at his dad. "We brought coffee and donuts. They're in the kitchen. Do you have time to hear about how I proposed? It was awesome."

Spencer laughed. "It was pretty epic."

"We want to hear everything," Hendrix said. "Give us ten minutes to freshen up, and we'll join you downstairs. Okay?"

"Sounds good." Preston took Spencer's hand, and the two of them left the office.

Hazel put her arms around Hendrix's waist. "Our boys are getting married."

Hendrix wiped away the tears on her cheeks with his

thumbs. "They are. Do you think they'll demand a double wedding when we tell them we're engaged?"

Hazel laughed. "Oh God, no."

Hendrix grinned. "I am ridiculously happy for them and us. How about you?"

"Over the moon." She stood on her tiptoes and pressed a kiss against his mouth. "I love you, Hendrix."

"I love you too, Hazel."

Keep reading for an excerpt from book two, "Take a Chance on Me" in the Seasoned Romance series.

TAKE A CHANCE ON ME EXCERPT

"Wait, where are you going?" Sierra's voice was cutting in and out, and Indie turned up the car volume before merging into the far lane.

"A place called Custom Rides. They do custom-built motorcycles," Indie said.

"Holy shit. Did your brother finally convince you to start driving a bike?" Sierra asked.

"God no, I am strictly a passenger when it comes to motorcycles. But it's his birthday in a couple of months, and Dad wants to get him a custom paint job for his bike. Dad found this place online and asked me to check it out since he's still in Arizona for another month.

"The store doesn't have a website with pictures of their work?" Sierra asked.

"They do, but you know Dad. He thinks everything on the internet is fake." Indie laughed. "So, now I'm driving across town on a very snowy Tuesday evening to a store where I'll potentially be the only woman and will either be completely ignored or have to suffer through a bunch of patronizing bull-shit from the store employees."

"Sound like a great time," Sierra said.

"What are you doing tonight?" Indie asked.

"Same thing I do every night... sanding, painting, and questioning why I ever thought buying a fixer-upper to reno-vate was a good idea," Sierra said.

"Because it was your dream, and now that your asshole of an ex-husband is out of the picture, you can live that dream?" Indie said.

Sierra laughed. "That is true. Hey, did you know that DIY drywalling is incredibly difficult? Like, I'm gonna have to hire a drywaller, difficult?"

"Sorry, honey," Indie said. "I know you really wanted to do everything yourself with the house."

"I do, but I also know my limits, and drywalling is one of them. None of your clients at the vet clinic happen to be reli-able drywallers with good reputations, do they?"

Indie laughed. "I don't think so, but I can double-check."

"Thanks, babe. Listen, I gotta go. The floor in the guest bedroom isn't going to sand itself. Love you."

"Love you too, Sierra."

Sierra ended the call, and Indie stopped at a red light, studying the snowy landscape. She'd ask one of the clinic receptionists about the drywalling thing. In her client appoint-ments, she rarely focused on anything beyond the animal she examined. Their owner's occupation wasn't a topic that usually came up.

You know what Val Jensen does for a living.

As usual, just the thought of the big, rough looking mechanic made her feel too warm and like she had tiny gymnasts doing backflips in her stomach. Val had come into the clinic with his daughter's pet bunny a few weeks ago, and despite his rough appearance, he'd had an obvious affection for the rabbit.

The robotic voice of her GPS told her to take the next right, and Indie flicked on her turn signal. She'd been immediately attracted to Val, and despite knowing someone like him would have no interest in someone like her, she'd made a fool of herself. She cringed as she turned right. God, the look on his face when she'd given him her cell number made her want to sink through the car floorboards, even though it'd been days since her humiliation. He'd seen right through her pretense that it was in case his rabbit fell ill again, and he hadn't called.

She sighed and drove carefully down the snowy road. She needed to stop thinking about Val Jensen and his dark eyes and granite body and those big, tattooed hands of his that she couldn't stop wondering what they'd look like cupping her breasts.

Indie, give it a rest. He's not interested in you, and you're gonna wear out your freaking vibrator if you don't stop fantasizing about him. I know you miss sex, but if you want a real dick and not that piece of plastic you hump every night, you need to stop fantasizing about the unattainable and find yourself a real-life fuckbuddy.

Inner Indie was right, but finding a guy who was only interested in sex with her once or twice a week had turned out to be much more difficult than she thought. Scratch that. Finding a guy who turned her on and could make her come was more difficult.

You're being too picky. You don't need to have a connection with the guy to fuck him. Hell, you don't even have to have a conversation with him.

Right again, but apparently, as much as she wanted to be the type of person who could just fuck someone regardless of whether she felt a connection or not, she wasn't. Her inability to come with the five guys she'd slept with since her divorce had proven she needed a connection. At least, she hoped that was the reason she couldn't come. She'd had a connection with her ex-husband, and there were plenty of times she'd had to fake it with him. But was she really asking for that much? Why was it so damn difficult to have an orgasm with a man? As much as she told herself it wasn't her, that she had some trauma from her ex blaming every issue on her, she still had a hard time believing it wasn't her fault. Her besties, Sierra and Hazel, had no problem orgasming with a guy, but here she was… forty-five years old and still struggling to have a great sex life.

Hell, forget great. She'd settle for a solid nice at this point.

The GPS announced the destination was on her right, and Indie turned into the Custom Rides parking lot. She parked and shut off her car, staring at the building in front of her. It was large with red siding and white trim. Two garage doors, painted white to match the trim, were on the left side of the building, and to the right was the front glass door with a dark grey awning over it. The Custom Rides logo was printed on the awning as well as on both garage doors.

Only one other car was in the parking lot, but warm light spilled out from the glass door. She climbed out of her SUV and walked to the building, checking the sign. They were open for another fifteen minutes, and she pulled open the door and stepped inside. The bell above the door jingled her arrival. Directly in front of her was a long counter set on top of a glass display case. The case held various motorcycle parts, each one shiny clean and gleaming in the light. A cash register sat on top of the counter, along with a small spinning stand holding Custom Rides keychains and an array of stainless-steel water bottles with the Custom Rides logo.

On the wall to the right, long metal pegs held a variety of Custom Rides merchandise, including shirts, hoodies, trucker hats, and vests. A door marked 'employees only' and a floor-to-ceiling display shelf of motorcycle helmets was at the back of the store. To her left was a large showroom with over a dozen bikes showcased. She walked over to the closest motorcycle, trailing her hand across the leather seat and along the metallic blue body.

"Holy shit," she murmured. While not a motorcycle expert, she knew more than the average person thanks to her father and brother's obsession, and she knew quality work when she saw it. Every bike in the showroom showed a master's touch, and she couldn't wait to tell her father he'd found the perfect place.

She touched the leather grips on the bike's handles before moving to the next motorcycle. This one was painted cherry red, and the chrome had been cleaned until it gleamed in the overhead lights. She ran her fingers along the seat, picturing what it would be like to be on the bike, her arms wrapped around the warm solid bulk of the man in front of her, her knees gripping his hips, the solid rumble of the bike's motor between her thighs.

She squeezed her thighs together. The only thing she missed about her dirtbag of an ex-husband was his bike. They'd gone on plenty of bike trips during their marriage, and she missed it with a fierce ache. So much that she'd even considered taking motorcycle driving lessons, but in the end, she'd chickened out. As much as she missed being on a bike, she really had no desire to learn how to drive one.

Maybe Val would take you for a ride on his bike.

She scoffed inwardly. Forgetting she'd never see him again, she had no idea if Mr. Valerie Jensen even drove a motorcycle. Sure, he looked like he did, but looking like he might be perfectly at ease on a bike, didn't mean he would be. Still, adding a detail like Val driving a motorcycle would certainly make her fantasy about him tonight a little richer. It wasn't like it harmed anyone to pretend that he drove a bike and would also be willing to bend her over it and fuck her into the best orgasm of her life. It was a harmless little fantasy that would give her beleaguered vibrator a real workout tonight.

She heard footsteps behind her, and then a shockingly familiar voice said, "How can I help you tonight?"

Indie froze, her fingers pressing hard into the leather seat. It couldn't be him. He was a mechanic. It was probably someone else with a honey-rough voice she couldn't get out of her head.

"Ma'am?" Now the voice held a hint of impatience. "Can I help you?"

Her body weirdly numb, and her breath whistling in and out of her lungs, Indie turned around. She stared at the big man behind her, at those pretty dark eyes, and big tattooed hands and the broad chest covered by a dark blue t-shirt with the words 'Custom Rides' etched into the material.

Her voice embarrassingly breathy, she said, "Hello, Mr. Jensen."

Val stared at her, his eyes widening just the tiniest bit. "Hello, doc."

ABOUT THE AUTHOR

Elizabeth Kelly was born and raised in Ontario, Canada. She moved west as a teenager and now lives in Alberta with her husband and a menagerie of pets. She firmly believes that a person can survive solely on sushi and coffee, and only her husband's mad cooking skills prevents her from proving that theory.

For more information about Elizabeth, check out her website at

www.elizabethkelly.ca

facebook.com/EKellyBooks

twitter.com/ElizabethKBooks

instagram.com/elizabethkelly_author

amazon.com/Elizabeth-Kelly/e/B00EOHZ0MS

bookbub.com/authors/elizabeth-kelly

ALSO BY ELIZABETH KELLY

Tempted Series

Tempted

Twice Tempted

Forever Tempted

Breathless

Tempted Trilogy (Books 1-3)

Red Moon Series

Red Moon

Red Moon Rising

Dark Moon

Alpha Moon

Pale Moon

The Recruit Series

The Recruit (Book One)

The Recruit (Book Two)

The Recruit (Book Three)

The Recruit (Book Four)

The Recruit (Book Five)

The Shifters Series

Willow and the Wolf (Book One)

Ava and the Bear (Book Two)

Katarina and the Bird (Book Three)

Porter's Mate (Book Four)

Bria and the Tiger (Book Five)

Rosalie Undone (Book Six)

The Dragon's Mate (Book Seven)

Rise of the Jaguar (Book Eight)

The Draax Series

Reign (Book One)

Rule (Book Two)

Rebel (Book Three)

Surrender (Book Four)

Harmony Falls Series

Sweet Harmony (Book One)

Perfect Harmony (Book Two)

Forbidden Harmony (Book Three)

Redeeming Harmony (Book Four)

Seasoned Romance Series

Bet Your Heart on Me (Book One)

Take a Chance on Me (Book Two)

Individual Books

The Necessary Engagement

Amelia's Touch

The Rancher's Daughter

Healing Gabriel

The Contract

A Home for Lily

Saving Charlotte

Shameless

The Fairy Tales Collection

Broken

An Unlikely Seduction

Holiday Romance

The Christmas Wife

The Christmas Rescue

The Christmas Nanny

The Christmas Boss

Sordid Games

Spencer turned slowly, staring first at Hazel and then Hendrix as Preston grabbed Hazel's hand. "Are you and my dad dating, Hazel?"

"No, we aren't… that is, we're just…."

"You're just screwing him to try to weasel your way back into my life," Spencer said.

"Watch your mouth," Hendrix said.

"Hendrix, don't," Hazel said. She reached for Spencer's hand, flinching when he stepped back like she was on fire. "Honey, this has nothing to do with our relationship, I promise. Hendrix asked me out before we even knew who the other person was and -"

"And you couldn't wait to use him to get close to me again, could you, Mom?" Spencer said. His voice rose, and Hendrix could see tears in his eyes. "I was worried when you didn't text me back last night. Preston and I went to your house, and when we realized that you drove to the cabin anyway, I spent most of last night freaking out that you were hurt. Because you're my mom, and I love you, and because I thought you had changed. I thought you knew I needed to live my own life, that I couldn't have you constantly in my face, demanding to be a part of everything that happened in my life, no matter how intrusive or inappropriate it was. But you haven't changed a bit, have you?"

"Honey, I have. I swear. I had no intention of sleeping with Hendrix, but -"

"But you did," Spencer said flatly. "You weren't happy with what I was offering, and you knew the fastest way to get back into my life was by sleeping with Preston's father. You knew how much Preston liked you and that he wanted a mom. You took advantage of him and his dad because you're obsessed with me. Do you know how sick that is, Mom?"

"Enough,' Hendrix snapped. "You have no idea what you're talking about, Spencer."

"No, *you* don't," Spencer said. "You think you know my mom, but you don't. She's using you, Mr. Smith. She's using you to get to me because she doesn't understand healthy boundaries and never will."

"Spencer," Preston said. "Your mom isn't -"

"Don't take her side," Spencer said as tears flowed down his cheeks. "I can't stand it if you do, Preston."

"I'm not," Preston said. "I love you, Spencer, and you know I'll always have your back. But give your mom a chance to explain, okay?"

"Explain what? How can you be okay with being used like this? With your dad being used by her?"

Hazel's face was a shade of white Hendrix didn't think skin could go. She swallowed hard, her voice shaking when she said, "I know you're upset, Spencer, but I swear that -"

"Stop it. Just stop," Spencer said. "I don't want to hear your lies or excuses, okay? Do you have any idea how gross and disturbing you are? Dad was right, you know. You'll never change. You smothered him, and when he couldn't take it anymore and left, you started smothering me. You need help, Mom. Serious help."

"Are you fucking kidding me?" Hendrix said. "You aren't -"

"You need to leave," Spencer said to Hazel. "I don't want you here."

"It's not your house," Hendrix said. "You don't get to make that decision."

"Fine," Spencer said before swiping his hand under his nose. "I'll leave. Preston, I'll see you at home."

"No, wait!" Hazel grabbed Spencer's arm, flinching again when he yanked his arm out of her grip. "I'll leave."